The
country
cottage

a prairie creek romance

ELIZABETH
BROMKE

May 1

W arning! #longpost ahead. You might want to grab a bowl of popcorn and a cuppa for this one, homesteaders...

This is not the post I was planning to make today.

I was *planning* to put up a pretty picture of my kitchen on this crisp Texas Monday morning. I was *planning* to show you my ivory farmhouse sink and cream-colored dish towels. My Simplify would peek from the shelf, and everything would be just as it always is. White and calm and me.

I was *planning* to do a post about how to start the week off right, with a farm-fresh breakfast and a clean kitchen and the perfection you've maybe come to expect from me...

But instead, here is my reality. A laptop with too many tabs open, half of them news sites. A plastic tumbler with

Diet Coke. A basket of unwashed laundry on the dining room table and smudges on the windows.

I. Am. Not. Okay.

By now, you know about *what happened.* *So, I'm not here to rehash anything. I'm here today to apologize. To my fans, I wish I hadn't let you down. To my family, I love you.*

To the Hayfields, I don't know where to begin. I'm sorry.

And to everyone, goodbye.

For now.

#homesteadandhearth #kellywatts #homesteaddreams #authenticity #reallife #illbeback #blessthismess

Chapter 1 — Kelly

K elly Watts sat on the edge of a white washed wood chair at her farmhouse table. To her left, an untouched iced coffee turned watery. To her right, an untouched egg-white omelet congealed on its blue-trimmed plate.

Directly in front of Kelly glowed the screen of her laptop. She gnawed on her bottom lip and scrolled through article after article. Each one read nearly identical to the last. The common message was simple, yet none of the reporters had gotten the whole story right. Just the most tantalizing bits.

Kelly glanced up to watch as Kyle moved into the kitchen, impervious to their collective fallout.

He was dressed in his usual—a hoodie better suited to a teenager than a forty-year-old, black nylon joggers, and neon tennis shoes. His head was freshly shaved and black-frame glasses perched neatly on his nose. Kyle was everything that Kelly was not. And yet their images had paired nicely up to now. She, the apron-clad, beautifully mussed Midwestern farmer's daughter. He, the new-age crypto guru. Kelly and Kyle. The perfect modern couple.

Or so everyone thought.

She combed her fingers into the roots of her hair, grabbed them and tugged hard. The self-inflicted pain did nothing to release the throb to her temples. Neither did rubbing hard at the tender skin in little circles. She collapsed on the table and sighed loudly. It was meant to capture her fiancé's attention, but he was either too glued to his phone to notice or the volume of his AirPods was too high for him to hear her.

Kelly lifted her head and eyed him. "Kyle." He didn't so much as flinch and continued his work of waiting for the espresso machine to drop its last drips. Kelly repeated his name, louder this time. "Kyle."

He more than flinched now. He nearly flung his phone out of his hand, jolting dramatically at the surprise. "Geez, Kelly." A scowl formed on his mouth. "What?"

She did not apologize and instead waved her own phone screen at him. "Have you read any of this?"

"Any of what?"

Kelly cleared her throat and intoned contemptuously, "'*Social Media Darling's Fall from Grace. The Story of Kelly Watts.*'"

"Who gives a—?"

"Or what about this one?" She read on. "*Bitcoin Babe*

Blows Up. The Implosion of an Internet #momboss." Kelly blinked and looked up at him. "We don't even have any kids."

"And we never will, which is exactly why you should be ignoring these trolls."

"Trolls? They're reporters. This one writes for *America Weekly*, Kyle. It's not like it's coming from the depths of some random web forums. This is headline news. *We* are headline news." She resumed scrolling until she was about to throw up from shame. "What am I going to do?"

The question was rhetorical, in fact. Kelly's team and the board at Homestead and Hearth were already working damage control from the company headquarters in Austin. Her only job right now was to stay home and out of the spotlight. That meant no posting, no texting, not even any phone calls to friends or family. The last thing was easiest. Kelly's only friends were already in the know. Kyle, obviously. Her personal assistant, Deb. And the rest of the team at H&H.

"Here's what you do," Kyle replied, stopping at the table on his way back to his in-home office at the other end of the house. She'd invited him to move in the winter before, but he was relegated to his own single bedroom for all things crypto or business. Kyle, too, had a workspace in Austin, but he rarely reported to it. Everything Kyle did could be handled at home, which Kelly thought she'd love. But it turned out crypto chic clashed with modern farmhouse and all things Kelly's brand. "You ignore it, and you wait. People's memories are short."

"Tell that to every single person who was ever canceled by popular media," she huffed.

Kyle's sympathy was as short as he figured people's memories were, apparently. He returned to his phone and wandered out.

In effect, all she really could do was wait. Wait for her PR manager to call with the plan. Wait for Deb to show up with chocolate therapy.

Wait for people to forget and forgive.

Chapter 2 — Logan

A shrill bleating woke Logan from his deep, dreamless sleep. The phone in the kitchen, an old red rotary, was all but shaking its receiver clear off when he arrived there to disengage the dang thing.

"Hello?" he mumbled into the line.

"Hi." The voice was twangy and piercing, and he hadn't had enough coffee to deal with more condolences yet. Especially if they were coming from an out-of-towner. "Is this the Ryersons'?"

Logan's great-aunt Melba had passed the week before, and it was her little country B and B that Logan was handling. No thanks to his sister, Mabel, who'd arrived for the funeral and left just a day later. If Logan was responsible and even-keeled, Mabel was a free spirit. She couldn't be counted on to come home to handle family members. She had a deep-seated grudge with half of the Ryersons. So, all that fell to Logan.

The person on the other end had allowed for a long pause.

Logan realized this was his cue. "Yes. Melba Ryerson's." He cleared his throat and rubbed at the stubble along his jaw, waiting for the gush of apologies to come. Melba had no shortage of admirers or friends. That had become clear over the past several days.

"Oh, I'm sorry. I must have the wrong number," replied the twang.

This woke Logan up a little. "The Ryersons'," he confirmed. "Melba Ryerson. You called about her passing, I'm sure."

"Her passing? Oh my word. No, no. I got this number through a hotelier connection out of Minneapolis. Did Melba Ryerson run the Ryersons' Cottage?"

Logan untangled the phone cord and tugged some slack to the nearby breakfast table. A little two-seater Melba had kept in the old kitchen there.

Although the forty-year-old had expected to take over the business, it seemed a little soon for any action. So far as he could tell, Melba hadn't had guests at the place in weeks. In many ways, Ryersons', as the little cottage inn was simply called, reminded Logan more of the Bates Motel than of a quaint country B and B. No doubt she had to work to draw in any business. But here was one such opportunity, landing squarely at the door. Or, on the phone, as the case may be.

"Yes, Melba owned and ran it." He felt a little foolish to be fielding the call now. Should he grab a pen and paper? Did Melba have a website where they could register or book a room?

The woman on the other end had the same questions, clearly. "And you are—?" she asked.

"Her nephew. Sorry. I'm Logan. I'm taking over for my aunt. I—um—you see, she was sort of a one-woman operation. We're scrambling to get things back in motion now." He squeezed his eyes shut and shook his head. Who was *we* anyway? Melba was a one-woman operation, and now Logan would be a one-man operation. Was he entirely crazy to think he could make this work? Keep the family property alive alongside his great aunt's dream?

Pft.

"Oh, of course. I'm terribly sorry. I'd hate to inconvenience you. Surely there's another little inn somewhere up there. If you have any referrals...?"

"No, no. I'm open. We're open for business. We're, er, I'm taking reservations. Happy to book a room or two for you."

"Oh, that's *wonderful*." The shrill twang returned, and Logan was reminded he still didn't have that pen and pad or a website or a guest registry or ledger or whatever he'd need.

A lot of other questions bubbled up, too. Where did Melba keep the fresh sheets and towels? Was there bacon in the fridge? Did she cook breakfast for everyone? More? If this woman wanted to book soon, how soon?

And, what did Melba charge?

Probably not much. Logan didn't need much anyway. He didn't need anything in fact. Financially, you couldn't do much better than owning a contracting business in the height of the market. Plus, he was a wise investor. So, if he didn't need the money, then why *was* he doing this?

For family. For a chance to come home and stay there.

And, because so long as Logan wasn't in Minneapolis, he wasn't near the memory of Delilah. No, he wasn't near other eligible bachelorettes either, but...

Anyway, Logan could distinctly recall his own mother complaining about how Melba lost more money than she made on the old country cottage that once belonged to the original Ryersons. The ones who'd come over from Denmark by way of Ellis Island. That's just how old this little place was. "I've got to admit, I'm winging it a bit here. Um, what dates are you looking at?" Logan spied a wall calendar hanging next to the phone and a pencil attached by string, almost magically.

"We're fairly flexible, but *soon*."

"Okay, so—next month?" He could pull off a lot in a month.

"Ack," the twang replied. "Sooner."

"Okay, how about a coupla weeks?"

"What about tomorrow?"

Deb dropped a rose gold Moleskin notebook on Kelly's desk.

The surface was entirely clear now, the staged mess eliminated an hour earlier. The whole house was clean, and Kyle was safely tucked away in his office at the other side of the house. He was packing it, ready to return to his condo in the city, which had better internet anyway.

"What's this?" Kelly stared at the fresh rectangle that lay askew on her repurposed vintage farmhouse table, white washed to oblivion. Just to the left rested the nexus of Kelly's world: her computer. It was there she wrote her blogs and produced her live videos and organized her entire life. It was to be her final moment with her smart phone and her computer, and Kelly felt unprepared.

Before Deb had dropped the innocent slab of pages

onto the table, Kelly had been studying the last image she'd crafted for her socials.

A square image of her in-home office, all of it perfectly pastel and beige and white and a touch shabby-chic and tastefully modern farmhouse and *so Kelly*. So *Homestead and Hearth*.

A perfectly crafted low-fat latte sat on a neat shiplap coaster to the left of a rose gold laptop.

On the right, a wireless mouse, centered on a custom mousepad, beige. Across the bottom, the company emblem: a white farmhouse—the sides of which made a capital *H*.

It was originally scheduled to go live on Tuesday for #TackleItTuesdays. But ever since Sunday night, Kelly had canceled all posts across all platforms.

And yet, though the posts were canceled, the images remained.

"This" Deb tapped on the front cover—"is your new Facebook. TikTok. Instagram. Twitter. Snapchat. FlipFlap. And whatever other blog and vlog comes to be in the month that you'll be offline."

Kelly lifted an eyebrow and slid a finger beneath the flap, opening the notebook to the first clean page. "How do you buy ad space for a *physical* journal?"

"We don't."

"So, what's the point?"

"This isn't for *Homestead and Hearth*, Kell. It's for *you*." Deb gave her a soft look and squeezed Kelly's shoulder. "From me."

For the first time since the scandal broke, so did Kelly. The floodgates opened up, and out came every last bit of emotion that she'd bottled up since she started her business, her brand, her new way of life. Because maybe what she'd built—from her ranch to her brand on down to her sweet assistant—was more than just a business. Maybe some of it was personal, too.

Chapter 3 — Kelly

Kelly watched as Deb worked her magic on the poor innkeeper on the other end of the line. She imagined it was a homely little woman in a tattered apron with curlers in her hair and the sort of heavy-looking eyeglasses that made a person look like a bug.

"That's *terrific!*" Deb all but shrieked into the line. Then, she put a hand over the receiver and whispered flatly to Kelly. "*We're in.*"

"*For how long?*" Kelly whispered back, though she already knew. She knew all the miserable details from the contract she'd just signed. Her board officially named it the *Save Kelly from Being Canceled Contract*, and she didn't find it funny.

"Do you have limits on reservations?" Deb asked on the phone.

The innkeeper must have been confused.

Deb explained, "How long can we book for? Is a month out of the question?"

Kelly chewed her pinky nail. It was her go-to chewing nail for occasions such as this. Even though she kept her manicures low key and neutral, it did no one good to spy the clear cut sign of stress on a woman who, by definition, could *Do. It. All.*

That was the *Homestead and Hearth* mantra.

Kelly Watts, the modern midwestern farmer's wife. She cooks. She cleans. She decorates. She primps (but it's all natural, baby!). And in her free time? She produces off-the-cuff, relatable, endearing videos to share with all those adoring internet fans, thereby sealing her authenticity as a true femmepreneur. A #momboss if she were a mother. A high-earning executive with lady parts. Did we mention she can do it all?

Deb slid an uneasy look at Kelly. "Here's the thing of it, Mr. Ryerson—"

Mr.? Kelly made a face. A man-innkeeper? And in South Dakota of all states?

Deb twisted away and launched into her best sales pitch, a winning-but-tasteful summary of Kelly's predicament complete with the one thing every average Joe in America would light up at. *Celebrity.*

"You see," Deb said, dropping her tone noticeably, "I'm the personal assistant for a high-profile client."

A pause.

Deb turned around and winked at Kelly, then went on, "Mm-hm, yes. She's, well, yes, she is well known the nation over. Anyway, Mr. Ryerson, we're looking for a quiet, out-of-the-way retreat up north."

Another pause.

"Well, there's been a personal event in her life and she needs to get away. Rest. Recover."

Kelly gasped and made wide eyes at Deb before mouthing, *I'm not a drug addict!*

But Deb waved her off and made some more hums and murmurs until finally she said, "No, she won't be using a pseudonym for this excursion. A big part of her goal is to come back down to earth for a while."

Annoyance crept beneath Kelly's skin. How Deb had found this place was luck, but it wasn't panning out. Obviously, there had been a death and this male innkeeper wasn't ready for prime time. Kelly made a slashing gesture across her throat. Just forget it. They'd find somewhere else. There must be a million little country inns.

Deb went on talking. "Her name is Kelly Watts." A pause. "Yes, that's her celebrity name." Another pause. "You might know her from her Homestead and Hearth collection? Or social media?" Faint panic spread over the assistant's delicate features. She looked at Kelly guiltily, but the expression faded away as soon as it came. "Actually, it's sort of perfect."

What's perfect? Kelly mouthed.

Deb confirmed the dates and address, thanked the man, then ended the call. A mischievous smile spread over her mouth. "He has no idea who you are."

Chapter 4 — Logan

After confirming the accommodations for Ms. Kelly Watts, Logan found his curiosity piquing. Maybe he should give the woman a good old-fashioned Google. Maybe she really was famous. And if that was the case, Logan might have to move back to the big city after all. Living under a rock was no way to meet women, after all.

Logan went for his phone in his pocket only to realize he was still in his pajamas. The phone was upstairs on its charger. Maybe his curiosity wasn't that powerful, because a wide yawn overtook him. He eyed the coffeepot in the corner of the kitchen counter. It was a restaurant-issue number with orange trim and brown paneling. Straight out of the seventies, probably the last time Melba had made any upgrades to the place.

The thought of going out and purchasing a brand-new coffee machine and everything else this place would need to continue to function was a daunting one. Then again, Logan *could* leave. He *could* go home. But what was home? A condo on the third floor of some shapeless building in downtown Minneapolis?

Nah.

Logan would stick around. For the summer at least. Probably longer. Anyway, his operations back in the city were on pause indefinitely. The crew already found other projects to tide them over. Logan's contracting business was all his own. No one to answer to, especially between jobs.

A rap came on the kitchen door—a makeshift butler's entrance, as if this place had been a mansion. This detail was something the original Ryersons would have added back when the cottage was more than a cottage. When it was a fully functioning dairy farm. Way back when.

Logan hollered an easy "Come in!" then set about digging out coffee grounds, a filter, and hitting the button to brew the coffee. As he did, the door opened and in popped Miles Gentry, Logan's best friend growing up and still to this day.

Logan grinned wide. "You're up early for a Saturday. What? I take it no one's biting down at The Gulch?" The Gulch was a Prairie Creek original. Back in the day, early settlers set up a whiskey still along Moccasin Creek, at the very southwest edge of town, way out of the way. One thing had led to another, and the still turned into a drinking hole which turned into a tavern. Another of their friends had bought it some years back. Now that's where Miles and every other single (and married-but-irritated) man in town spent their Friday nights.

"Ha. Ha." But Miles wasn't laughing. "I'll take one of those." He grabbed a mug from the rings hanging beneath a cupboard and indicated the percolating coffee. As much time as they'd spent at one another's houses growing up, the boys had spent even more here, at the Ryerson cottage. There was room to roam, animals to chase, and wood to cut. Plus, back in the day, Aunt Melba was quite possibly the best cookie baker north of the Mason-Dixon line.

Definitely the best in Prairie Creek. The boys would know. They worked for cookies back then—raking leaves, trapping prairie dogs, all that.

"It'll be a while. This thing is older than you and me."

"Not by much. I feel like I remember when she bought it. That was the time when your uncle got sick. Remember? Aunt Melba sold off the animals and started letting rooms."

"Yeah." Logan stretched his back against the counter, his muscles tightening from one short week of a *lack* of physical labor. When you were around forty, it turned out you got just as sore from sitting around as you did from hauling lumber and wielding power tools. A thought came over him. "Hey, have you ever heard of a *Kelly Watts*?"

Miles grabbed one of several covered plates from the

icebox, lowered at the table and pulled it up to him. Casseroles, pies, platters, and treats of all types littered the place. People who'd come to Melba's funeral had expected to find children or grandchildren shattered like broken glass in the wake of her death. But they weren't close enough to know that Melba had no children. And the family who were left behind, well they were shattered, all right. But in a different way. In the way where there was no one to argue about inheritances or what the woman's last wishes had been. No one to sob into a stranger's shoulder and recount that one time ol' Melba ran out to the yard in broad daylight in her dressing gown to shoo a deer out of her garden only to turn around and invite the wild animal into her mudroom for a drink and a bowl of grits.

"Kelly Watts?" Miles had tucked into day-old meatloaf and spoke with his mouth half-full. "You mean Kari Watson—sure. She was a grade above us. 'Member?"

"No, not Kari Watson. Kelly Watts. She's not from Prairie Creek."

"Where's she from? Aberdeen? Milbank? I think there's a Watts clan in Sioux Falls. I know there is—they're cousins, I'm pretty sure."

"Miles, she's a celebrity."

"A celebrity?" Miles stopped chewing, and a lump of meatloaf could be detected in his chipmunk cheek as he grappled for his phone from his shirt pocket. "Why do you ask?" He was already looking her up. "Ugh."

"I know. It's slow."

"Do you even have high-speed wireless internet?"

At that, Logan laughed. "There's no internet at all. You're working off of your phone network there, buddy boy. Same as me. It'll be a few minutes before anything comes up. *If* it ever comes up."

"I got an idea." Miles stood and moved to the phone then pushed his finger into the little plastic wheel, pulling seven numbers around. "Lucy, hey." His sister, of course. Lucy Gentry was a spoiled twenty-something who'd been nothing more than a pest to Miles and Logan when they were teenagers. She was a little girl back then, and sometimes it seemed like she never did grow up. "Do you know who this woman is? She's famous, I guess. Her name is Kelly Watts. Not Watson, *Watts*."

Logan could literally hear the shriek come over the line. There was no use in either one of them trying to make sense of Lucy's screeches, so Miles spoke louder over her. "Lucy. Lucy! Just send me a picture, will you? Okay? To my cell."

She must have made a smart remark because Miles rolled his eyes.

"Whatever, just send it. A text'll come through faster than I can get this internet to work." He fell silent while he listened, and after a moment looked at Logan. "She wants to know why we're asking." Then, Miles handed the receiver over to Logan.

Logan froze up. He was pretty sure the assistant-lady had mentioned something about an NDA, and Logan didn't know much about celebrities, but he sure as heck knew a lot about the world. At least, for the small-town boy he grew up as. He grabbed the phone and sucked Lucy's excitement out of her like a car wash vacuum. "Aunt Melba had a picture with her autograph on it. We want to make sure it's really her."

Then, he hung up. Even though Lucy had begun to freak out all over again.

"So, why *are* you asking about her?" Miles asked, returning to the meatloaf.

"I just got off the phone with her assistant. She's booked a room." Logan returned his efforts to the coffee situation.

"Where?"

"*Here*."

May 3

Day 1.
     I can't remember the last time I wrote in a diary. My online posts don't count, do they? But I guess that's the closest I've been to sitting down and writing what I'm thinking and feeling.

The only thing is I'm not sure how I'll do this without adding hashtags. Maybe I'll put them down anyway. #no
Ugh.

This morning, we leave for Nowhere, USA. I can't say I'm dreading it. I can't even say I'm dreading leaving Kyle. I know he's not dreading my leaving. He was all but giddy when he said goodbye today and told me if I needed "more time" to take it! Go ahead, Kelly! Leave forever!

But forever isn't the plan. Just for now is the plan. Anyway, I know Kyle's opinion doesn't matter. Sorry, but I'm not that sorry.

Deb said I could write down anything I need to in here.

24

She said if there's something I can't tell her, I can write it here. But there's nothing Deb doesn't already know. She knows the truth. She knows the lies, too.

I guess that leaves me to fill these blank pages with something else. Like, the in-between. The stuff in the middle of truth and lies. The stuff that I haven't figured out yet.

Chapter 5 — Kelly

Everything was set. Or, as set as they could get, considering the fact that this was to be a low-tech, off-the-grid type of situation.

The company paid for a private jet to avoid any shred of publicity or tabloid dodging. Later, if the plan unfolded as it was supposed to, Kelly would film a series of shorts in a rented vintage van (*#vanlife*) to suggest she'd hit the road, Jack; she'd traveled the road not taken; she opted for the rocky road. All those metaphors to prove Kelly had some sort of transformation to go through.

Even though she definitely did not. The scandal was pure rumor. Gossip. Slander, even.

But in this day and age, any celebrity worth his or her weight would grovel and take the blame. So Kelly would take it. She'd take it all.

Deb made the voyage alongside Kelly to the classically small town of Prairie Creek, South Dakota. There, they would lie low together in the very out-of-the-way cottage named Ryersons', as if it were a department store. Little about the destination made sense to Kelly, despite having grown up in a small town herself.

They each stared, Deb and Kelly, out their respective windows. "Did you grow up in Austin, Deb?" Kelly realized how precious little she knew about her assistant. It was a flaw in Kelly, to have missed those opportunities for inquiry. Perhaps a symptom of her overnight fame. She cringed inwardly and looked at the pretty-but-plain woman, with shoulder-length chestnut hair, curled under simply but smartly. She wore silver wire-rim glasses, and though Kelly *did* know Deb's age—fifty-one —Deb was the sort to appear either closer to thirty or closer to sixty, depending on who you asked.

"Nope. I grew up in Albuquerque. It's kind of like Austin, though." Deb adjusted her glasses. "Guess we were never too far away from each other, even growing up, huh?"

Kelly considered this. "I guess not. Arizona and New Mexico are kissin' states, anyway. I didn't realize you were from ABQ, Deb. Did you like it there? Why'd you move?"

"Same reason as you, I guess. To see the world. I bounced around only to wind up in a place that was pretty familiar, you know?"

Kelly returned her gaze to the window. They were landing now. She didn't really know. Sierra Vista was a military town. She'd gone to a public high school where new kids came and went. Transient was a word she'd learned at a young age. Her mother had taught it to her. Mamie Watts had always said *Why travel the world when you can bring the world to you?*

"They're not as great as movies make you think," Kelly murmured while the flight crew set about deplaning procedures.

"What's not as great?" Deb was already on her tablet, swiping left and right and up and down, although Kelly had no idea what the woman could be organizing now. They had one mission and one mission only: to arrive quietly at the little country cottage on the outskirts of town.

But the conversation had passed, and Kelly didn't want to dredge up her old pains. "Nothing. Did you say we're getting a town car service?"

"Not exactly." Deb finished with her tablet and stored it neatly into the satchel she wore at all times. "Apparently, the little cottage is sending someone to get us."

"Oh. So, they've got a valet?"

"*Not exactly*," Deb repeated.

May 3

Day 1. Again.

It's funny, how from way up here Earth just cycles through colors and shapes. That's in between the clouds, anyway.

Deb tells me that she found pictures of the place online, posted by #roadtrippers and #seeamerica types. She gave me a glance and it's darling. Lots and lots of precious patchwork quilts and cast iron. It reminds me of <u>Little House on the Prairie</u>, in the best way. Now, if only the guy running the place is as handsome as Michael Landon.

Hah. Even if he is, I bet anything I'll have my work waiting for me back home in Austin. Even Michael Landon wouldn't stand a chance to break my concentration once I'm home.

Home.

Funny how "home" takes on a new meaning when your circumstances switch.

I wonder what Mom would be saying right now. Mom? Can you read this, up there wherever you're perching right about now? Can people in Heaven see earthly diaries? I hope not, because I shudder to think what Grandpa Watts would have thought about my teenage diary. Ick.

Mom, remember how you were so good at justifying our circumstances? You always said, Why travel the world when you can bring the world to you? That was the beauty in living near an army base. We got to sample other people and other places right there, at home.

Mom, I don't know if you had it right, though. Just because I happened to meet military brats with their ample experience at various national and international forts didn't mean I tasted much of the world. What it had meant was that I didn't know exactly where in the world I belonged. I wasn't a military brat. You were a homemaker. Dad worked for the postal service as a mail carrier.

But embedded in your adage was a seed of truth. The truth that there was nothing quite wrong with being at home. With loving what you have at home. In your own home. With bringing, perhaps not the whole world, but with bringing happiness into your home. With being happy at home.

The thing of it is, Mom, I'm not. Happy that is. Not at the ranch outside of Austin. Not at my home.

Chapter 6 — Kelly

After deplaning and retrieving their luggage—Kelly was forbidden from packing more than a single full-size suitcase—the pair moved across the private tarmac toward a truck that sat waiting nearby. Not a black limo or a white Escalade or even a Range Rover. A truck. And...it wasn't anything fancy, either. Big, yes. Fancy, no. Clean, kind of. Fancy, *no*.

Kelly exchanged a look with Deb. "This is the valet?"

"He's not exactly a valet."

"What? He's a serial killer?"

"He's *Ryerson*. The owner of the inn."

That was when Kelly spied him, getting out of his truck and looking nothing like a little Midwestern grandmother who let her rooms out to passersby. Oh no.

Well-built and tall, the man was dressed casually in jeans that could only be Wranglers, work boots tied loosely, and a white T-shirt. Over that, he'd thrown on a flannel button-down but had left it wide open, the sleeves pushed up.

As Kelly and Deb neared him, Kelly's skin tingled. Was it the dry air? The brittle wind that coursed across the asphalt and slipped a thatch of her hair over her face, obscuring her vision momentarily and tantalizingly?

She pulled her hair from her face and there he was all over again striding toward them now, easily. Smiling. Kind and tall and were those...*dimples*? And the rest of him. Chestnut hair and eyes to match. Sun-kissed skin, despite the nip in the late spring air. A shadow that crossed his jaw—stubble that Kelly had only ever read about in romance novels.

She forced herself to find something interesting about the plains beyond the little airport, because thoughts of Kyle prickled up into Kelly's brain.

Kyle.

Kelly's so-called fiancé. The one who'd had a chance to come along for the low-tech get-away but who couldn't possibly leave the so-called grid. Markets could crash. Markets could soar. Anything could happen, and he'd be entirely incapable of capitalizing or snaking his way out of a bad investment.

Kyle.

The reason Kelly was even in this mess.

Chapter 7 — Logan

Logan idled in his trusty blue Dodge for some time before the plane came into view. It was one of those private jets with a pilot in the typical aviators and headset staring stoically as he pulled the craft to a full stop and fiddled with switches. Logan hated to fly. He'd had his fill when he was in the military.

Soon enough, the crew opened the hatch and after a trio of flight attendants, down stepped two civilian-looking figures. He didn't have a close view from where he sat, so he pulled the truck up a little closer—as close as the TSA guys in orange vests allowed.

The first of the two women was notably shorter, sure-footed and practical, with transitional-lens glasses sitting on her nose and a brown satchel fitted close to her stocky torso, Logan liked her immediately. She reminded him of Melba, for some reason. Despite the wide age gap.

The other woman, though, had to be *her*.

Kelly Watts.

The famous one—or, *infamous*, as Logan had come to learn.Though could someone really be infamous if they weren't first famous? Maybe. He'd never know. And before this very moment, he didn't think he'd have ever cared, either.

Standing at around five-eight, maybe five-nine, he guessed, she probably came to his chin. Not thin, but rather strong-looking, she wore her body well. Confidence wafted about her as she easily accepted a large piece of luggage with one hand and flipped a sheath of long fiery hair over her shoulder. She wore oversize sunglasses, which was every bit the cliché. And a broad sunhat somehow didn't make her look dowdy, but instead, mysterious.

Logan unfastened his seat belt and hopped out of the truck.

"Hiya!" He waved and smiled in their direction. The practical-looking one sped up.

"You must be Mr. Ryerson!" she yelled more loudly than was necessary. They weren't at an airshow. Just the private lot out back of a smallish regional airport that was hardly on the aviation map.

"Call me Logan. Welcome to South Dakota."

Melba's mini-me stuck out a hand. "Debra Benson. Call me Deb." She hurried her friend along with a little wave. "This is Ms. Watts."

Logan wasn't the staring type, at least, he didn't think he was. But once Ms. Watts joined the pair, pulled off her sunglasses and hat and gave her long red strands a shake, he might as well have been drooling at a shampoo commercial.

Up close, Kelly Watts looked every bit the celebrity she apparently was. Creamy skin with a smattering of pale freckles. Full lips that hardly hid perfectly straight white teeth even though she wasn't smiling. At first.

Then, her eyes. Free of makeup and cornflower blue, those eyes could end wars. Logan's heart raced in his chest, and he felt his palms grow clammy. Instead of offering his hand to hers for a shake, he reached for her bag.

"That looks heavy. Let me help."

She let him take the bag but held his gaze. "Logan? You're the owner of the inn?"

"Ah—" He hesitated. How would it sound that he owned an inn? Wouldn't it be better to call the place a sprawling resort or mountain retreat or something with at least an edge of masculinity? The cottage wasn't that, though. So, instead, he managed, "It belonged to my aunt. She recently passed, and I'm stepping in for now."

"Oh." Kelly tucked her hair behind her ear and flicked an overt glance to her friend. "Well, we can't wait to get settled in. The pictures online are just darling."

Darling. Inwardly, Logan winced. "It's a family heirloom, you could say. Comfortable but—" His eyes trailed briefly down her body. She practically matched him. Jeans and a red flannel shirt—possibly men's. The sleeves were rolled up and it hung loosely from her body, but the silhouette of her shape persevered. Not a man's shirt. A woman's. Probably expensive. One of those numbers meant to look down home and casual but actually turned out hip and chic. Logan swallowed and forced his eyes up immediately. "Let's just say you might want to temper your expectations."

Her smile persisted. And then, she winked. "They *are* pretty high."

Chapter 8 — Kelly

It turned out the quaint blue truck was cozier than it looked. No king cab. No backseat.

When it came time to decide who'd sit in the middle (and therefore next to Logan), Deb made a face and whispered to Kelly, "It's indecent."

Logan was busy loading their bags.

"What do you mean?" Kelly whispered back.

"For me to sit in the middle. It would be indecent."

"Why?" Kelly stole a look at the bed of the truck. Logan was closing the tailgate, and even from that angle she could see sinewy muscles rippling in his arms. What was *wrong* with her? Talk about indecent. Sheesh.

"I'm widowed, and I'm older. It makes sense you sit in the middle. And anyway, I can film you." On cue, Deb pulled out the camcorder they'd been issued for the trip. It wasn't a smartphone—Kelly was forbidden from bringing a smartphone. This was a good old-fashioned video recorder. Deb was responsible for the camera and for documenting *everything*.

"Not this," Kelly protested. "You're not going to film me squished in the middle of you two as we bump along backroads through the Badlands."

"Nah." Logan appeared in the cab just as Kelly had opened the passenger door to gauge how much space they actually had. "The Badlands are in the southwestern part of the state. We're in the northeast."

"Right." She turned and glared at Deb, who couldn't seem to contain the twinkle in her eye. She and Deb climbed into the cab and Kelly made sure there was at least an inch between her body and Logan's. She didn't know him. He didn't know her. There was no need for their bodies to touch for a thirty-minute jaunt into the countryside.

He put the truck in gear and out they pulled.

But they came to a stop shortly after. Kelly thought the truck had stalled out. When she looked over at Logan, he had a sheepish expression on his face. "Sorry, I'm sort of a stickler for seatbelts. Would you two buckle up?"

Kelly had thought there wasn't a middle seatbelt, but she found it tucked along her right thigh and pulled it over.

Deb pulled hers on, too, and he got them going again.

The trio was on the road for not two minutes when

Kelly's thigh started to involuntarily shift to Logan's. If he were a gentleman, he'd scoot over.

"Sorry." She awkwardly tugged her middle seat belt loose and moved back toward Deb.

Logan looked at her from the corner of his eye. "Sorry about the truck. I'm sort of a one-man operation."

"It's fine." Kelly kept her eyes forward. And it was fine. They were here to rough it, and riding middle in a blue Dodge pickup fit the bill perfectly. Maybe Deb *should* be recording content right now.

As if their minds had melded, Deb pulled out the camcorder.

"Mind if I take some shots while we drive?" Deb asked.

Logan glanced over. "Oh, not at all." He looked edgy.

Kelly tried to assuage any anxieties. She understood. The camera could be intimidating if you weren't used to it. "Just be glad the whole film crew didn't tag along."

"Why didn't they?" Logan asked. "I had to sign an NDA and the production plan or schedule or whatever seemed *intense*." He lifted a skeptical eyebrow.

Kelly grinned. "I'm sure editing will be intense." Lots to fix in postproduction, she knew. That's how social media influencing *really* worked. Did people actually think Chip and Joanna and Pioneer Woman and Martha Stewart woke up looking like that? That they didn't flub on camera. And there was more to cut than bloopers.

There was dead air and boring sentences and awkward transitions.

Then, there was all the adding. The filters and added content. If Kelly were filming a day in the kitchen, baking, that content could be text overlay with recipes. If she were doing a décor piece on how to set a hearth, editing might add in the fire, depending on the location.

Then there were the bedroom pieces, often rich with innuendo. Kelly recalled a content piece her producers requested. It was a breakfast-in-bed idea where Kelly was supposed to pretend like she actually stayed in bed past four in the morning. Then Kyle would come along, dressed in Homestead and Hearth men's collection and carrying a Homestead and Hearth breakfast tray on which was poised a glass of orange juice, a plate of eggs, sunny-side up for effect (Kelly preferred scrambled), two thick slices of multi-grain toast each with a pat of butter and a side of two slivers of bacon (who could afford to eat bacon these days?).

Then, hidden in her needlessly and ornately folded Homestead and Hearth napkin would be the ring.

Mind you, Kyle had proposed to Kelly months before all this, but it took the team a while to brew up the proposal. They didn't like Kyle's spontaneous after-dinner private one. They needed something promotional and viral. A breakfast-in-bed surprise fit the bill.

Kelly rubbed the pad of her thumb on the underside of the ring now. Their engagement wasn't on hold. Not exactly. But as part of the package deal, Kelly had to agree to a think piece for the *Gazette*. "A Life Suspended: A Canceled Social Star Steps Away from the Spotlight to Fix What's Broken." The long title annoyed her. The implication annoyed her. And now her ring annoyed her.

But that was the thing. If Kelly had broken her engagement, she'd have broken the contract. Enough was broken in her life, the producers said. But they weren't interested in her staying around to fix things. Oh, no. She had to get out of Dodge. Out of the limelight. Out of the *way*.

But Kyle stayed. He wasn't their star. He was their pawn.

Then again, so was Kelly.

Chapter 9 — Logan

Logan figured the brief road trip was going as well as it could. He didn't mind driving and even less so when a beautiful woman was beside him. But this particular beautiful woman was also a guest at the cottage, and an undercurrent of tension throbbed along like an extra passenger in the truck cab.

He thought about something he could ask, but that NDA scared him. Logan was only to be as involved in this pseudo-documentary thing insofar as the Homestead and Hearth needed him to be.

"What's your place like in Texas? Is it a farm or a ranch or—?"

Kelly shifted away from him again, and each time she did that, he felt a twinge of betrayal. A ridiculous feeling, to be sure, but it couldn't be helped. He didn't mind that their thighs touched. Then again, there was a big fat diamond glittering on her finger. Anyway, his Google search revealed Kelly was engaged to be married. Maybe it was best she scoot away and their bodies kept to themselves.

Then, she relaxed. He felt the side of her body return to his. When he stole a glance, he saw her face light up. "It's a ranch. A real Texas ranch with a rambling single-level, split rail fencing out front, and a big red broadsided barn out back. It belonged to a family of pioneers and was passed down generation to generation. Just outside of Austin, if you're familiar with the area." She didn't stop to learn if he was, but he was. Logan was stationed at Fort Hood for a time. "We refurbished it slowly. Before I did home décor for a living, I was a home economics teacher. That was back when home ec was still a thing in some schools, but it was a dying program even then. Anyway, as a teacher, I had no money. My mom helped me with cosigning a loan and cobbling together a down payment, though." She paused and he thought he heard her voice hitch a little. But Kelly cleared her throat and finished what she was saying. "We preserved as much of the original property as we could."

After she fell silent, Logan asked, "Is your mom part of your company, too, then?"

A throaty *nuh-uh* came in reply. A beat. Then, "She passed."

"I'm sorry." Logan quietly cursed himself. This was exactly why you didn't make small talk. Because small talk could lead to big talk and they weren't ready for big talk yet, even if they were stuck side by side in his truck for half an hour.

Even if they'd be stuck in the cottage together for a month.

Thankfully Deb knew how to handle the situation. "Kelly's mom was the one who pushed Kelly to follow her dreams. We all have her to thank for the company. From the board members on down to the chickens."

"Chickens?" A chance for redirection. Logan snatched it right up. "Like, real chickens? You keep livestock?"

Kelly's voice turned wistful. "I wish we had more. For now, just the birds. I'd like to see the ranch take on goats and a dairy cow, too. Pigs. Maybe sheep one day? But I don't know anymore. And while I'm out here, I don't know what they'll do with it."

He cocked an eyebrow and looked at her. "*They*?"

A flat line settled over her mouth. "Once I sold Homestead and Hearth to Southwest Media Group, all decisions moved to them, even though I was the star, so to speak."

"So, you don't technically own your brand anymore? That's what it's called, a brand?"

"Something like that."

Again, Logan felt the outside of his right thigh cool as she inched away.

As if to steer the conversation elsewhere, Deb interjected brightly again, "So, Mr. Ryerson—Logan, I mean —tell us about the cottage."

"Sure, yeah. Well, there isn't much to tell. It's got five bedrooms we use as guest rooms. There are just two bathrooms, which can be awkward. I wasn't around much the last decade or so, but way back when I remember Melba saying she didn't mind that guests shared bathrooms mainly 'cause it meant fewer bathrooms to clean." He chuckled to himself over his practical aunt, but the distinct feeling that he'd made a misstep crept over him. "And the kitchen is separate from the dining room, which I know has become passé, but that's how it was built."

"When was the place built? Did your aunt Melba build it?"

"She's actually my great-aunt, and no. My great-grandparents built the cottage and ran the farm. Melba was my grandmother's sister. She and Uncle Ned didn't have kids of their own, so when Grandma and Grandpa Ryerson passed, it made sense for Melba to stay on and take over. Ned was a useful guy, but he was no farmer. More like a banker-type. The farm was hard on them, I guess. Soon enough, they rented rooms to make a living."

"And now it belongs to you?"

"Yes and no." He twisted his hands on the steering wheel as they veered off of the I12, exiting onto 281 South down to Prairie Creek. "I was close to Aunt Melba, and so was my sister. So, she left it to us."

"You have a sister, aw," Deb tutted. "I bet she lives just down the road."

"Not exactly. Mabel left town about a year ago. She's

ELIZABETH BROMKE

out of the picture. Family drama. You know how that goes." He really hated to get into the Mabel saga. "Anyway, since Mabel is preoccupied out west, it fell to me. I don't like the idea of selling off a family heirloom, so we'll see what happens." He shrugged. "Oh, but I guess you wanted to know more about the cottage itself. Not its history."

The rest of the ride south down the 281 was quieter. Well, Logan was quieter. Deb wanted to get footage of the landscape—the flat yellowy green that stretched on and on, interrupted only by the glimmering promise of a creek or lake here or there.

And she took some shots of Kelly, too. Logan lingered in the background of the footage, staring coolly ahead at the wide, open road. Just a couple miles until their next turn-off at 142nd Avenue. Then another few miles to County Road 33.

Then, they'd arrive at the cottage. And things would get a little more real.

"I have to warn you," he remarked once Deb had stowed her camera and it was clear they were getting closer. "The cottage is no Ritz Carlton."

Chapter 10 — *Kelly*

Kelly laughed at Logan's warning. He had to realize that they were *not* looking for a luxury five-star resort. "We did get a peek of the cottage online already."

He adjusted his hands on the steering wheel and cleared his throat. "I'm not sure what you would have seen. To my knowledge, the extent of my aunt's marketing was word of mouth."

"Oh, we searched your hashtag," Deb chirped away, entirely pleasant and happy to be along for the ride while Kelly's inner thighs were starting to burn from squeezing them together so as not to brush up against Logan again. The effort was futile now, though, because they'd left the highway for a crude country road—not dirt, but not maintained, either.

Logan tried to share a knowing look with Kelly, but you can't share a knowing look with someone you don't know. She pursed her lips and explained to him, "Hashtags are ways for people to sort of highlight something online. Make it easier to find."

He grinned. "I know what hashtags are. I didn't know Melba was a user of them." Despite his surly words, his tone was gentle and kind, and Kelly pinned him as being very opposite to Kyle. Which was just as well. She moved her hand to the spot beneath her thigh as if she'd find her phone there. It wasn't though. Any communication with Kyle would have to happen the old-fashioned way—via a landline, if the cottage had one. And then, Deb would document the call with a photo and a post to Homestead and Hearth's social accounts. Nothing was to be genuine on this trip. Except for Kelly's sacrifice of modern technology. That was *it*.

"Your aunt probably didn't use the hashtags. Visitors to her cottage did." Deb flashed her phone screen for Kelly and Logan to see. "Look, see? Hashtag Ryersons' Cottage. Hashtag Prairie Creek Cottage. Hashtag country inn. Hashtag country life. Hashtag down home. Hashtag—"

"I get it." Logan held up a hand. Kelly smiled. Deb could be a lot, but she always meant well.

"You must be busy with so much action over there." She cringed as the words rolled out of her mouth like marbles. It was all wrong. Her face and neck burned. "I mean with how much business your aunt's place gets."

He gave her a wry look. "Ol' Aunt Melba wasn't getting much action. At the cottage, *I mean*."

"Really?" Kelly was surprised to hear this and turned to Deb, expecting to share in the unexpected news.

But Deb's face twisted like she was about to burst into laughter. "And you?"

Logan looked first at Kelly then to Deb. "Pardon me?"

Deb wasn't that bad, though, and instead of asking what Kelly feared the sturdy bottle-brunette might blurt out, she softened the question.

At least a little bit.

"Business might be slow, but what about you? Are you a busy guy?"

"Just with the cottage now," he replied, suspicion creeping over his face, though it seemed that he tried to remain impassive. "I have a contracting business in the city—Minneapolis. It's on hold for now. I'm former military, so the pension plus savings will tide me over while I decide what to do."

Kelly turned to him. "You might not keep it?"

"The cottage?" Logan shrugged. "We'll see. Seems like business is thin out this way generally, not just at my aunt's." He jerked his chin straight on and Kelly followed, taking in the narrow stretch of roadway that split the spread of flatlands into two. Before them lay miles and miles of prairie, and it occurred to Kelly in that moment that there was lots of beauty to be had in this neck of the country. And, this was another unexpected thing.

"That's why I'm here, though," Kelly said. "Because no one else seems to be."

* * *

Logan took them off the single-lane road and onto a dusty, old dirt lane. The truck bumped and thumped along, and he assured them they were only another ten minutes away from the farm.

It was hard to have a smooth conversation on such uneven terrain. Each person was more concerned with keeping the center of his or her mass, well, central. The effort to do this about toppled Kelly's resilience. How she longed to unclench her torso and legs and let her body relax entirely. But there was little relaxation to be had, even on a one-month getaway that was supposed to be anything *but* relaxing.

"There she is." Logan, whose wrist lay limply over top of the steering wheel, pointed ahead.

The farm came into view, but just barely, like a wobbly image created not in reality but in the promise of something more than reality.

Like hope.

Chapter 11—Logan

Logan saw the farm through Kelly's and Deb's eyes. As an underwhelming red bungalow with shabby white trim, wildflowers a little too wild —he knew they looked more like weeds except for that one particular spell Kelly had happened to book herself there.

He rolled slowly down the dirt drive, past a broken wood fence with a wagon wheel resting up against one side. Stopping out front in a clearing used as a little parking lot, he shut off the engine and popped open his door. Instead of following Deb, Kelly scooted his way, behind the wheel and after Logan, and he was quick with a hand to help her out.

"Easy there," he said, realizing he'd better run around to help Deb, too. But by the time Logan had unhooked himself from Kelly's pretty gaze beyond him and up at the cottage, Deb had already hopped out and pulled her own smaller piece of luggage from the bed of the truck, too. She was a tough little woman, and once again gave him flashbacks of Aunt Melba.

"I can get that for you, if you and Kelly want to explore?"

Kelly whipped around, her hair blowing off of her face. "I think we were hoping for a tour, actually. We can get the bags later, right?"

Deb added, "You two go ahead. I'll hang back and film."

"Film?" Logan was already growing tired of the documentary thing. As if their stay here was going to amount to something worthy of sending back to Hollywood producers. He highly doubted it, but Kelly's attitude lightened, and her smile and wide eyes and easy body language told him to go along with it.

So, he did.

"All right."

Kelly and Logan walked side by side, and he pointed out little things like the water well, and how his great-grandpa Ryerson dug it himself. At least, that was family lore. They passed the pigpen, which was positioned unfortunately at the front of the farm. Logan didn't know why they wouldn't have hidden a thing like a pig pen, but there it was, a split-rail fence with wire mesh separating the grass from a big square of mud, perfect for rolling in.

"When was the last time you had pigs here?" She asked this question seriously, and Logan glanced back at

Deb, who trailed behind by just a couple of yards, her camera poised and rolling, apparently.

"Should I be talking to *you*?" He pointed at Deb, but she waved him off.

"No, no! I'm not here! You two just do what you're doing."

Logan dropped his voice and leaned closer to Kelly. "What *are* we doing, exactly?"

She turned her head to answer him, maybe unaware how close his face was to her ear, and they nearly bumped noses. But Kelly just laughed, her perfect teeth and freckled face shining in the sunlight.

Logan tried to swallow a lump that formed in his throat, but it wouldn't go down. His chest felt hollow and his breath short, and he worried he'd start panting or something equally humiliating. "Sorry, I didn't mean to get in your bubble there."

Kelly smiled back. "Isn't that what we're *doing*?"

Chapter 12 — Kelly

O nce again, she hadn't meant to spit out an innuendo. It just kept happening. Logan was good looking and sweet natured, and normally Kelly would be uncomfortable around that sort of guy.

She chewed her lower lip as he fumbled with a confused response. "Well, the cottage is small, but not that small. You'll have your own rooms, each of you. I have my own space, too, and well—"

A force deep within Kelly lifted her hand to his shoulder and squeezed it. Almost as if she were speaking to an adoring fan, someone who craved her touch and who she felt the distinct need to reassure and comfort. "I know. I just meant that we'll probably be bumping into each other here." She sighed and looked up. They stood in front of the most precious little house she'd ever laid eyes on. Sure, it was a bit rusty in some spots—withering paint and a loose shutter here or there. Windows that needed a good cleaning. But beyond all that, Kelly saw the one thing that could save her hide.

That was, if she wanted her hide saved. "Logan, do you have a telephone I could use?"

He went for his pocket, and she shook her head. "Like, a landline?"

"Oh, um. Sure. Sorry, yeah. Just in the kitchen, I'll show you the way." He again looked around at Deb, who'd hung back at a metal water pump station. It was as though they'd fallen into the year 1900. Deb was eating it all up as much as Kelly. They shared a longing for the past. That's what made them great at their work—homesteading, and teaching others about it. And caring for the home. It was an art form that had taken a hit with the dawn of women's rights and women's entrance into the workforce. Not that Kelly would ever want to go back on that whole movement—she treasured her vote and her voice—but there was something to be said for keeping the home fires burning, the beds warm, a hot meal waiting for a family. Kelly longed for all those things, and that was why she'd built up the company she had. As a way to have what felt impossible in this maddeningly, wonderfully modern age.

She was on her way, too. Not just with the company, that had already blown up—good and bad, now. But in her personal life. Her wedding was just around the corner. The producers asked Kyle and Kelly to expedite the date so that it could function as a season finale for her vlog after this little retreat up north. Kyle and Kelly would reunite amid an ocean of white roses down at the ranch outside of Austin. That was the plan, anyway. Who knew what would transpire between now and then.

"Okay, well, here's the porch." Logan rubbed the back of his head. "It's, I guess it's just a covered porch. The roof is shingle." He pointed up above their heads, but the overhang wasn't particularly interesting. Everyone's gaze fell back down. Kelly studied the little white rocking chair that swayed as they moved over creaking wooden planks. Her examination of the quaint outdoor space continued around as though this was a house she might flip.

Affixed over the front door was a storm screen door, aluminum metal and mesh and dated at least fifty years. Its condition was impressive, considering. So, too, was the condition of the siding here. In South Dakota, Kelly imagined snow was a beast against wood. It was any wonder this whole place wasn't shingled over or sided in metal to help stave off damage from wind, rain, and snow.

She turned though, reminded of a long thatch of crops that lined the house and property on almost all sides save for a space at the end of the drive, to allow for access, of course.

Turning back to the cottage, she imagined what would be inside. Shabby chic decor? Or remnants of a family who survived the dustbowl? Cobble stone floors like something out of the French countryside? Or sturdy, handcrafted and waxed wood floors, more common, regionally. Then again, it could surprise her. Maybe the woman who'd just passed had treaded shag carpet and linoleum. There was nothing wrong with easy upkeep and comfort, after all.

Deb, who'd rejoined them now, hissed at Kelly, "Talk about your observations, Kel. I know you're taking *everything* in."

Kelly wished she weren't here for work. She wished she really could disappear into rural America, never to be heard from again. But if she did that, she'd have to kiss her money goodbye. Heck, she'd have to kiss everything in her life goodbye. It was one thing to fantasize about disappearing. It was another to be forced into a pretend version of it.

The public might think Kelly Watts was hiding out in some underground bunker in Alaska or something, eating grits for three meals a day and practicing self flagellation for some heinous personal truth that had come to light. In reality, she'd be living in the very type of little house she decorated for the camera. And she'd still be on camera. Not using her own devices, maybe, but the whole de-technification of her little *time-out* was all pretense.

Kelly was beginning to wonder what elements of her life were *not* pretense.

Ⓜay 3

We made it, and it's...not what I expected. Well, let me back up. The cottage is exactly what I expected. Even better.

The red-painted clapboard siding pops out from white trim and gray shingles. Edges along the porch beams and at the seams of the house are worn, and it needs a little work just about everywhere. The windows are a bit cloudy, but not from grime necessarily. More like from age, the good kind of cloudy. I know. Windows should never be cloudy. I'm crazy. But I like it. It reminds of antique glasses, like the passage of time has collected in slim films over the glass, making it hard to see in if you're standing away from the house and squinting. Not always a bad thing. Sometimes windows aren't meant to look in through. They're meant to look out of. That's how the cottage windows are.

Inside of the tidy, narrow porch, the foyer is small and

designated solely by a small square table with an oil lamp on top and a dish for keys next to it. The front desk, if you can call it that, is beyond the staircase, which unravels down from a cramped second floor. It would appear the front desk was carved beneath the staircase, like maybe it used to be a cloak closet or a mudroom for little feet that had just spent the morning jumping through puddles.

Logan's desk, or rather Melba's, I guess, is as old as the cottage, probably. Maybe Melba dragged it home from a local antique shop. It's a heavy, dark wooden thing. Behind it, close to where the innkeeper manages the ledger, is a cubby shelf with five keys dangling from five hooks. One for each guest room.

Another lamp, this one electric with a green glass shade, spills yellow light over the desk top, worn with age and the elbows and forearms of those who've signed in and checked out over the years.

The kitchen is off to the right of the foyer, and it belies the turn-of-the-century heaviness of the staircase and front desk. Maybe there had been an update to the home in the forties or fifties? I spied hints of both decades. White and black checkered laminate flooring. A big white sink spread across the back wall, with built in grooves to let dishes dry on. The cabinets were painted white with red trim and complemented the flooring too perfectly for words. If I were to take on this project for a reno or a redec, I'd do little. Otherwise, I'd risk losing the charm.

The rooms. Ahhh. Again, expectedly adorable. All quilts and hardwood flooring covered over in tartan rugs.

Rocking chairs and sideboards with lace doilies and basin stands adorn the edges of each bedroom. I feel like I'm in Amish country.

I love it.

But...

What I did not expect was everything else. The pang of loneliness. The missing my mother, who'd have cherished this little country place. The longing for a life that isn't mine in a world to which I don't belong.

I did not expect to feel so...sad.

May 4

Breakfast is wafting up to my bedroom. Cynical me is wondering about the insulation of the interior walls in this house—or lack thereof.

Pleasant me, the dominant force of late, is loving every little nuance of this place.

I'll have to call Kyle this morning and check in on his final two closings. I mean, they're Brenda's now, but Kyle still has a little skin the game. This is his final go. The end of an era. A brief era, but an era all to its own. The era of me trying to share my business with my "fiancé"

Also the era of me being engaged.

Yep, you heard it here first. Oh, wait. No one is reading this. So nobody knows. Well, Deb knows. That's it. If I had a best friend, she would know, but the price of fame is such that best friends come in the form of assistants and managers, the latter of which I no longer have.

Sometimes, I wonder if Kyle really knows. Actually,

scratch that. I wonder if I know. I miss him, but in the way I missed a pet hamster I once had for two years. Having the hamster was more often a pain than a joy, but Pippy, my little tawny-haired rodent, had her moments. Mostly it was the early days, the excitement of having a pet all my own. We didn't have a lot of money then, sure, but we had scraps around the farm, so you can bet I made her obstacle courses and mazes and adventures. But the newness turned to nuisance, and her escapades escaping overnight only for Mom to scream bloody murder the next morning, well, those got old real fast. So did the stink of her cage. And then the time she had a litter of baby hamsters and tried to eat one before I swiftly intervened.

Come to think of it, having Pippy for a pet was all work and little play. All worrying, all justifying. "But, Mom, I DID latch her cage, I swear!" and "I know she's my responsibility, but I'm tired. I'll clean the cage tomorrow."

Tomorrow always came too soon with Pippy.

And so it has been with Kyle. Especially after the scandal.

I could have pinned it on him. It was his fault, anyway. But Kyle was smarter than that, and just as soon as we got news of the tragedy, he wined and dined me like the early days. I felt like Pippy, as he promised me this, that, and the other in order to keep him out of the picture. He had a bigger empire, he argued. He had more to lose. None of that really got to me, though. I'm not dumb.

What got to me was his cool logic. The fact was, even if

I'd tried to pin everything on Kyle, I was still to blame. The buck stops with me. At my company, even; despite the board of supervisors, the public thinks I call the shots, and if there is a misstep in my brand, ultimately, it belongs to me.

And so, I agreed with Kyle, but I'm not dumb and I'm not a doormat. I told him I'd play the hideaway game and go off. But he would finish his projects for H&H and then allow me *to announce the dissolution of our engagement.*

Yep.

The public might cancel me, but at least I get to cancel Kyle.

Chapter 13 — Logan

"Hi!" Logan was busy with breakfast when the two women descended the stairway the next morning. He could hear them before he saw them, and his greeting was met with wide yawns and sleepy eyes. "You two like pancakes and bacon? It's sort of *the* breakfast around these parts."

"Pancakes." Kelly grinned. "Do you know the last time I had home-cooked pancakes for breakfast?"

Deb added, "When you made them on Easter Sunday. Or were those crepes?"

"Crepes." Kelly clicked her tongue and added playfully, "It's hard to get those two confused, Deb."

Deb gave a wry smile. "True, especially since crepes are better."

"Pancakes are better," Logan and Kelly said at the exact same moment and with the exact same cadence and

Logan wasn't even sure if Kelly had actually said it, because their voices synced so perfectly.

But her look of surprise confirmed that they had, and he was quick to tack on, "Jinx." Then pointed at her. "You owe me a Coke."

Kelly cocked her head and her smile widened. "I haven't heard that in forever."

"Which part? Jinx or You owe me a Coke?"

"Both."

Deb set about filling mugs with coffee. "Well, Kelly, when was the last time you shared the exact same thought with someone?"

At this, Kelly's smile fell away as she bit down on her lower lip and hooked a finger toward the wall. "Logan, mind if I use your phone?"

He gave the long-corded red receiver a funny look and flipped a flapjack before shrugging. "Have at it."

Deb said, "It'll be long distance, and the production team will reimburse."

"I'm not sure I remember the last time I made a long-distance phone call on a landline." Logan studied the bacon that sizzled in his aunt's cast iron skillet. It was about ready.

Meanwhile, Kelly picked up the receiver and mouthed *Thank you* before slipping around the corner and disappearing into the hall.

Logan watched as the phone cord pulled and pulled until Kelly must have moved all the way across the foyer and into the small sitting room on the other side of the house. It was a long phone cord. It could carry her into total privacy.

Deb must have read his mind. "I'm sure she's calling her fiancé." She said the sentence with a sourness, and the nettling look on her face invited him to respond.

"Fiancé? I didn't realize."

"You didn't see that gaudy ring on her finger? He got her a size too small, so it's not like she can get it off even if she wanted to." Then, Deb dropped her voice. "And trust me, she *wants* to."

Logan wasn't sure what to do with this revelation. Did he rejoice? Play it cool? Inquire further? The spirit of his great Aunt Melba must have overtaken him, because he sidled up closer to Deb, dropped his voice low and said, "Why?"

Deb scoffed. "Kyle Fatalny is *not*—" But she stopped short and pretended to button her lips. "Never mind."

That was that, and Logan knew better than to push Deb. It was none of his business, Kelly's love life. Even if she was beautiful. Even if he was heartsick.

"How about you, Mr. Country Cottage? Where's the little wife with her apron and red lipstick?" Deb pretended to look around the place before taking a long pull of her coffee.

"Not here." He kept his eyes ahead.

"Must be a girlfriend somewhere. Back home in Minnesota, eh?" Deb tried for a midwestern accent but it hit weird and Deb laughed at herself.

"Yeah, well. Something like that." He frowned. Now wasn't the time to get into it.

"Oh, come on. You can tell me. I'm not filming right now. Sometimes it helps to talk through breakups." Deb meant well, and she really was soft and kind and she'd be a great person to open up to, but Logan wasn't there yet. Not with a sweet older lady like Deb.

Not with anyone.

Not even with himself.

Chapter 14 — Kelly

K elly wrapped the phone cord slack around her hand, twisting and untwisting. The very act was as natural as if she used a landline every day, but the last time she'd even been near a corded phone was probably twenty-five years ago. Maybe longer.

Kyle answered after several rings and probably just before he was about to miss her call.

Typical. She was calling from an unknown number, even though Kelly reminded him she'd *be* calling from an unknown number.

"Hello?" His voice was painted in suspicion.

"Hey. It's *me*." Kelly peeked through to the kitchen to see Deb nosing around in a cupboard.

Also typical.

"Oh, hi." No *Babe*. She was okay with that. "I thought it was spam."

"I told you—" she stopped short. "Never mind. How's it going? Any...news?"

"News?"

Was he playing dumb?

"Yes, Kyle. News about the news." She hated to even utter the word *scandal*. What happened was not a scandal. It was a misunderstanding.

He responded vaguely that he hadn't been online yet, which Kelly knew was a total crock. Her own attention to him ebbed when she heard an engine roar outside.

"Well, keep me posted. I hope you're doing okay." Her voice sounded hollow to her as Kelly looked through the high windows of the front door to see a lone, dusty sedan flip a U-turn. As he made his way back from where he came, he chucked something out of the driver's side window.

Of course. Kelly smiled to herself. The newspaper. A little late, maybe, but then, they were way far out. Couldn't blame the paperboy for that. Not in these parts. Not in this day and age where precious few even ordered a real, live subscription.

She started out for it just as Kyle replied, "You, too."

His voice sounded hollow, too. Or was it quiet? A whisper?

"Are you whispering?" she asked. She didn't mean to be paranoid or weird, but then wasn't he the weird one for whispering? Oh, who cared? It didn't matter anymore. She was in South Dakota. He was carrying on the façade back home. At least, he was supposed to be.

"What?" Now he was extra loud, oddly so. "No." A nervous laugh. Kelly knew that laugh, despite the fact that she sometimes wondered just how well she really knew Kyle. "*No*," he spat. The laughter was sucked from the phone line.

Even with Kyle's adamance that he wasn't whispering, his overall affect bothered her. She opted to move away from it, though. "How did closing go?"

"Coyote Trail or Mesa Point?"

Kyle had only joined the flipping side of Homestead and Hearth six months before. It had been a mistake. And the two properties he still oversaw were the last he ever would. After he closed on them for Kelly, he was out of the brand.

For good.

"Both, I guess?"

Kyle cleared his throat. "Um, yeah. Mesa, we're waiting on the inspection report."

"You were supposed to get that yesterday, I thought." Anxiety roiled in Kelly's stomach. She couldn't afford any more drama. She was trusting Kyle to keep things tight and locked down.

"The inspection happened yesterday. I'm pretty sure. Listen, Kelly, I have a lot on my plate. The new coin drops this afternoon. The team is convening at the downtown offices, and I have to actually be there in person. It's a huge deal, Kelly. The property sales are the least of my concern right now."

"Well, they are the most of my concern." She wanted

to cry. But something stopped her. "What new coin?" When a new cryptocurrency was about to come out, it was all Kyle ever talked about. She hadn't heard a single thing about this new one.

"Uh, yeah. It was a huge secret project, and we just learned about it. So, I'm heading into the city, and I'll be out of touch the rest of the day, FYI."

FYI. Kelly sighed. "Okay. Well, I'll call Brenda to take over on the sales, then." This was Kelly giving up on Kyle. At least, in terms of their fleeting business partnership.

"That'd be tight."

Tight. Was he fifteen?

She sighed again. "Make sure if you get *any* correspondence from the buyers' agent that you forward it to Brenda. You have her email. Right?"

"Listen, just go relax, Kelly. That's what you're up there to do, right? Spa days and self-care?"

"Something like that." She let Kyle hang up first, until she heard the distinct and nearly obsolete sound of a dial tone in her ear. Then she stared out at the miniature gray lump that lay in grassy weeds a hundred yards off.

A quick skip back into the kitchen to return the receiver to its cradle revealed that breakfast was nearly ready.

"Have a seat. Flapjacks are about done."

Kelly pointed back in the direction she'd come from.

"Actually, did I just see a paper get chucked up the drive?"

"A paper?" Logan swiveled with a spatula in one hand and his coffee mug in the other. "Oh, the newspaper. Yeah. I'm pretty sure Melba stopped paying for it a decade ago, but it keeps coming."

"Mind if I bring it in?"

"Do I mind?" He grinned, and Kelly once again saw that kind twinkling in his eyes. The shadow across his jaw and the Adam's apple and the cleft in his chin and again those twinkling blue eyes. This was going to be a long, painful month. "Heck, I'll knock a few bucks off your bill. Can you milk the cows while you're out there?"

Kelly lifted a playful eyebrow. "I'll slop the pigs while I'm at it."

Logan and Deb chuckled as Kelly left through the screen door in the kitchen and plodded along the dirt path to where the newspaper lay about fifty yards from the road. Newspaper boys these days. Pfft. Then again, if this was a freebie or a local periodical, it could be that she was about to arrive at something no thicker than a coupon mailer.

But, no. It was a real, live paper, complete with a quaint title that, once she un-rubber-banded and unfolded the thing, read, *The Prairie Gazette*. The cuteness just kept on coming.

As she made her way back into the cottage, Kelly let the paper open and she skimmed the headlines. They weren't like big-city headlines or even the ones from the smaller journals out of Austin. They were sweet and upbeat. "Prairie Creek High School Spelling Bee Names Winner." And "Fire Chief Retires after 40-Year Career."

Kelly walked back to the cottage as she skimmed the articles, with their puffy language and down-home tone. She turned the page to find continuations of the first part, ads, and county news.

After that came local and state sports reports.

Then opinion.

After that were the classifieds, which took up a whopping two full pages. It was as though no one had learned about Marketplace or Etsy or Mercari yet. Then again, the sorts of things for sale in the greater Prairie Creek area probably wouldn't get much action on Etsy. Tractors. Doublewides. Firewood.

Job listings were few, which had to be a good thing. The local salon was hiring. Creek Cuts 'n' More. How darling. Custodian for Prairie Creek Public School District.

Obituaries fell between the job listings and lifestyle pages. This was where Kelly stopped short, little pillows of dust blew plumes at her feet as she halted and studied the biggest photo of the three.

Kelly's jaw dropped. Her heart sank. Her whole entire world crashed down.

Again.

Chapter 15 — Logan

Deb had already tucked into her short stack, but Logan refused to eat ahead of Kelly. What was the point of a bed and breakfast operation if the innkeeper ate all the breakfast before the guests?

He glanced at the clock on the wall, a cuckoo number probably dating back to WWI.

"You going to do any renovating here?" Deb asked between mouthfuls.

Logan licked his lips. "I'm not sure. I need to talk to my sister. I mean, she's out of the equation, truly, but I feel like that's more up her alley than it is mine."

"Aren't you contracting?"

"Yeah, so I could do the heavy lifting. Not the lace doilies, though. Or the booking stuff."

"Would your sister?"

"No, but, I think it'd need a woman's touch around

here is my point, and Mabel is the closest I've got to that." Then he raised an eyebrow at Deb. "Unless you see yourself making a home in Prairie Creek?"

Deb flushed red and giggled before shaking her head. "No, no, no. I'm a Texas mama. All my interests are back home down south." She lifted her face toward the door, and Logan followed her gaze to see Kelly with her nose buried in the paper. A man could dream, right?

"Looking for news about yourself?" Deb asked Kelly.

Logan smirked. "Doubt you'd find any in the *Gazette*. That thing is strictly read for school gossip, the police beat, and car accidents."

But Kelly didn't smile back. Her face was stretched in something akin to panic, or even anger. Logan's chest tightened. Had he said something wrong? Done something? Was she reading an article about him?

Couldn't be. Why would Logan Ryerson turn up in the *Gazette*, unless it was for the cottage or something, but that wasn't newspaper worthy. Not *yet*, at least...

Kelly looked first at Logan, and he saw something flicker in her eyes. A softness, like she might cry. Or was it...embarrassment? Had she actually made the *Gazette* after all?

"Um," was all Kelly could get out before her gaze moved to Deb, and the softness left it. Now he could see clearly what she felt was anger, directed squarely at the sweet, innocent woman sitting with a slice of bacon dangling from two fingers pinched together.

"I'll go," Logan interjected, smart enough to read the room.

Kelly didn't bother to reply to him, and Deb was frozen in place with her bacon in hand. Logan started to back out just as Kelly flattened the paper down on the table and stabbed a familiar picture with her finger.

"That's Mrs. Hayfield," he said, now curious.

Kelly glanced his way then stabbed the picture again. "Yes. It is. So, what in the world is she doing in Prairie Creek's newspaper, Deb?"

Deb visibly shrank in her chair.

But it was Logan who could easily answer. "She was a teacher here at the elementary school. Mrs. Hayfield. I had her in the third grade. Scared the living tar out of me. My mom almost put me on antidepressants as an eight-year-old just to deal with ol' Mrs. Hayfield. My buddies and me, we called her Mrs. Haymaker behind her back. Man, oh man. If we'd've ever got caught—" Logan braced for an impact that wouldn't come, but that was Mrs. Hayfield for you, an impotent but eternal threat.

"She lived here? In Prairie Creek?" Kelly asked.

Deb looked at Logan. "We didn't actually mention this to her."

"Didn't mention what to me?" Kelly demanded, nostrils flared.

Logan felt his face go hot. He *was* in trouble, but he hadn't done anything. What was Deb talking about? What was Kelly talking about? What did ol' Mrs. Haymaker have to do with any of it? "Can somebody please explain how you two know my third grade teacher?"

Kelly's face turned to stone. "We don't. I mean—not personally."

"She was a client," Deb added, but Kelly stared daggers at the poor woman, who effectively fell quiet. Kelly was a force. That couldn't be argued.

"Oh, you renovated her house? Is that what you do, by the way? Home renovations? It's a little like my career, actually."

Kelly sighed and pressed her mouth into a line. "You really don't know Homestead and Hearth? Or...*me*?"

At this, he took a long swig of his coffee, set it on the table, folded his arms and gave her a good, hard smirk. "Sorry, no. And I'd be honestly surprised if Mrs. Hayfield did. It's not you, it's *us*."

"Actually, over thirty percent of our viewership and followership hail from or currently reside in the north Midwest region of the contiguous United States. Thirty-four percent, to be exact," Deb offered weakly. "But of that thirty-four percent, women or people who identify as women make up eighty-six percent." She gave a nervous smile. "Chances are you had heard of Kelly Watts but weren't sure how you knew her. That's what polls would predict."

Befuddled, Logan scratched his head and reached again for his coffee. "Anyway, my condolences." He looked at the paper that lay as lifelessly as ol' Mrs. Hayfield.

"Again, we didn't know her personally. *I* didn't know her personally." Kelly stopped for a thoughtful moment. "You really haven't heard about this? About Joanna Hayfield, me, or *Homestead and Hearth*?" she asked Logan, her eyes searching hard into his like she might have laser vision.

"I really haven't. I'm sorry."

"Well, Joanna Hayfield had." Kelly looked balefully at Deb. "You knew, didn't you?"

Again, Logan had the sense to back out, but as he began to move toward the doorway and into the front hall, Deb pointed to him. "It was the cottage. Melba Ryerson. It just—it came together, Kelly." Deb crunched into a piece of her bacon and chewed it very slowly. "It wasn't my idea." Again she pointed at Logan, as if their trip to South Dakota *was* his idea, but it wasn't. Not by a mile. He hadn't even planned to open the cottage back up after Melba's funeral, for goodness' sake!

He raised his hands in surrender. "I'm not—I didn't even know who you were. No offense. And I definitely don't know what this had to do with Mrs. Haymaker—I mean Mrs. Hayfield." He glanced toward the paper with a purposeful look. "I hadn't heard she'd passed."

Deb lifted the page with Mrs. Hayfield's picture and accompanying memorial paragraphs. For being as mean a lady as she had been, somebody had put in a nice word for her. Several nice words, by the length of the thing. And having just done an obit himself, Logan knew it cost a pretty penny to say so many nice things once a person died. Deb tapped the woman's face. "This person is the reason we're here." She looked at Logan then at Kelly. "There, I said it. It's out. Now you two can figure out where that puts you."

"Where that puts us?" Kelly said exactly what Logan was thinking, and they exchanged a look of confusion. "What do you mean, Deb? You tricked me. Leave him out of this. Obviously our gracious jailer has been living under a rock for the better half of the millennium!"

"Do we still call it that?" Logan interrupted gently. "The millennium. I mean, we're over two decades in now, and so—" he stopped, the smile on his face creeping up higher and higher.

Both women looked at him. He was treading on thin ice, but if he was going to wade knee deep into some reality-star, celebrity drama, then he might as well poke some fun where he could.

The women's looks, however, told him he'd just crashed through that delicate layer between air and frigid water.

Again, he raised his hands. "Maybe if you tell me why you really came here, I could better appreciate what my third grade teacher's death has to do with everything and how I can help you. *If* I can help you."

Deb stood abruptly from the table, her pancakes mostly remaining. Her second mug of coffee, too. Only the three strips of bacon she'd slipped onto her plate were totally gone. She wiped her hands on a little white paper napkin that Logan had rustled up from deep inside a cabinet. "I'll tell you what happened with planning this thing," she dipped her chin to Logan, "if you tell him why in the world you're hiding." And with that, the portly brunette left.

Logan finally took his place at the table and picked up his fork and knife, pointing with the latter at Kelly's plate and the two porcelain jars of condiments that sat nearby. "Maple syrup or strawberry?"

Chapter 16 — Kelly

Kelly sat with a thud and hooked her pointer finger to the syrup, her preference. "I can't tell you why I'm here. Not if you don't already know, Logan."

He pushed aside his coffee and folded his arms. Each time he did this, she couldn't help but notice once again how different Logan was than Kyle. Not that Kyle didn't lock his arms across his chest—it was a common enough thing for a person to do. Hah. But because of the little things about Logan. His red flannel shirt, only slightly different from yesterday's—or was it? The sleeves pushed up without a care for detail. His forearms thick and sinewy in muscles that only certain men used. The kind of men who swung power tools around and climbed rafters and balanced on ladders. The kind that Kelly was used to seeing on her sets and at her project sites, but then...there was something else. Logan wasn't only muscle and bunched shirt sleeves. He was soft, too.

"I don't understand, Kelly. Why can't you tell me? I mean, I know we don't know each other, but everyone has a past. That's what this is about, right? Something from your past?"

Kelly closed her eyes. She *wished* this whole thing were in the past. Or that the public's discovery of it was in the past.

"It's just—I don't know." She stabbed a square tower of pancakes with her fork and shoved it into her mouth, relishing the sweet, buttery flavor, the soft texture, the everything-ness of actually getting to eat down-home food rather than just prepare it for a camera and promptly schlep it over to the production crew. She swallowed and took a long gulp of coffee. Logan continued to watch her and wait. She raised her hands up and pushed away the rest of the plate of pancakes and returned Logan's stare. "Okay, here's what I can say. 'I was doing great. Then, something happened. Your teacher, Mrs. Hayfield, was involved in a peripheral way. The public blamed me, and when the public blames a media figure for something in this day and age, it doesn't just go away. They get canceled. The only way to recover from such a fate is to go away and repent, then come back and make up for it all. So, that's why I'm here.' Satisfied?"

He pushed the plate of pancakes back to her and dove into his own, but then he shook his head. "I still don't know what ol' Mrs. Hayfield has to do with it all, but I'm getting closer. I mean...she is dead." Then he looked up, a jeering smile on his face and a glint in his eye. "Did you murder her?"

In spite of herself, Kelly laughed. A full-bellied laugh that drew her hands to her face, which had absolutely flushed bright red and *not* because she had murdered Mrs. Hayfield. "No!" she protested before slapping her hand over the table and toward him. Why was this so easy? With Logan, a perfect stranger?

"So a mean old lady died, you had something to do with it—according to gossip-rag readers—and now you're here. At my cottage." His jeer turned sweeter. "I'm not complaining."

The rush of blood in her cheeks didn't ebb. In fact, she felt her neck burn up, and the roots of her hair tingle. Was he...*flirting*?

"But you *are* wondering what Mrs. Hayfield was doing down in Texas, with me." She looked down at the plate of buttery, syrupy goodness and took Logan's cue to keep at it. She was back on a farm now, a real one. Not a ranch with white shiplap and rose gold accents. A farm with doors that didn't lock—the shared bathroom, for example. If there was any one place in the world Kelly didn't have to worry about her macros and micros and carbs and sugars, it was here, in the country. At this little cottage. She could all but feel her very own grandmother's sweet voice singsonging to her, "Cookies, Kelly! Cookies for my little Cookie-Eating Kelly!"

"She retired, according to this." He thumbed the obituary.

"Retired down to Texas. Why couldn't it have been Florida?"

Logan shoveled the last of his pancake into his mouth and started in on the bacon. "I was starving."

"No housewife around to keep you fed?" She was flirting, too. Shamelessly, but who cared? Not Kyle. Not Deb.

But the question, or her tone, had struck him wrong, because Logan's face fell, and he ran a napkin over his mouth before working up something to answer with.

"Sorry, I was joking. I'm a housewife type. It's not offensive to me." Was he that sort of guy? The type who fought aggressively for a woman's equal rights to get out of the kitchen and into the cubicle?

No. That wasn't it, because what fell out of Logan's mouth next was nothing short of stinging. "Nope." He gave her a stony look. "Not anymore."

May 5

I'm scared to go downstairs, but I can't hold out much longer. It's been all I can do to skip breakfast today and steal away to the bathroom only when absolutely necessary.

Yesterday was a bust. Deb hid from me, taking the truck into town to do some footage-gathering. Logan seemed mad about my housewife joke. Is he divorced? Or is there a bad breakup in his recent history? He didn't say more after the awkward breakfast, and then lunch was declared make-it-yourself. Dinner? Pizza by delivery, which ended up taking two hours to arrive, and by then it was cold.

Logan apologized after, and I did, too. Obviously I messed up somehow, but I can't take it. Not the silent treatment and not Deb running off for a whole day up to the nearest city. Aberdeen. Cute name. I'd have liked to go, but then once we sat at the table to dive into the pizza, Deb wouldn't make eye contact.

I can't very well text her from my bed. All I have is this diary. I mean, I guess I could tear a sheet out, scribble a note and shove it under her door?

WHY IS EVERYONE MAD AT ME?

That would be childish, and I'm not a child. I'm an adult, taking her consequences with grace and humility. It's just that...I don't need more. What happened to Joanna was enough. Right? Punishment enough? Punishment for getting too big for my britches, as my dad would say.

Punishment for trusting the wrong guy, as my mom would have said.

Oh, Mom. Can we just pretend that these pages are your ears and heart? Your eyes? That you can see me and feel me and hear me and that you can pick up a pen and reply? Remember how we did that one summer? I wrote little passages in my diary, and then if I needed you to know what was going on, I left it on your bed. Remember? And you'd write a note back.

Remember the one where I got in such big trouble I couldn't barely stand to wake up in the morning? Looking back, it was such a silly thing. Okay, I'll remind you. I was fifteen, and our volleyball team played against this big school out of Tucson. They even brought their own mascot. I never knew high schools had mascots. I guess we had one, too, but—anyway. My friend dared me to pull the tail. I did. It ripped. I ran.

The coach threatened the whole team. Spill who did this or everyone earned three days of straight conditioning. I broke down immediately, of course I did. I sobbed and confessed and sobbed some more. I remember going into the girls' restroom after and I looked in the mirror, and the girl looking back wasn't me. She had different colored eyes, and her cheeks were all red and smeary. Her freckles glowed red like zits, and her hair was soggy and limp. It was like the worst of me had been living inside only to crawl out finally with this pesky little bad decision.

It blew over, for everyone else. I lived with the guilt of what I'd done and the pain from the humiliation for over a month before I took to that diary and wrote down every-thing that happened. I spared no details, and when I was done, in the wee hours of some morning, I tiptoed into your bedroom and quietly left it on the foot of your bed.

I went to school and wondered about you and my diary all day. I kept waiting to get called to the principal's office where you'd be waiting, fuming. I kept waiting to be dragged out by the ear and screamed at and slapped. But you never did those things before, so why my fear? I guess there was some deep-seated rule-follower inside of me that wondered when you'd break from the compassionate kind mother into the witchy one I'd read about in fairytales.

You never came. Instead, when I got home from school that day, you'd returned my diary. Inside of it, you wrote (and I'll never forget this): If that's the worst thing you do in your life, I'd say you're in good shape, Sugar.

Well, Mom. I've done worse by now.

Much, much worse.
What would you say to me now?

Chapter 17 — Logan

Come Wednesday, the jig was up. Logan realized he wasn't cut out to host guests at the cottage. He was a joke of an innkeeper, and he was longing to do something more than whip up pancakes and bacon and put on a happy face.

Melba's death dredged up other rough memories. Keeping it a secret from Kelly and Deb started to feel like a struggle, despite the fact that they *should* enjoy a little distance. He wasn't vacationing with them. They weren't running the cottage with him.

First, he called his mom. This was her sort of territory, the cottage and the women. And anyway, Mabel was only barely replying to her big brother's texts. She was so checked out of things, that he didn't want to go there.

"Logan! When are ya coming home?" Nasal though

it may be, Logan's mother's voice was a comfort. But *home* didn't feel right, for some reason. Yes, Nance and Norm Ryerson lived in Minneapolis like Logan. They'd decided to find a nice patio home there. Something small and low-maintenance with good insulation. "Are ya really going to stay on with the cottage? You know you have yer dad's permission to give it up, don'tcha?"

Yes, he knew. This wasn't about his dad and the man's lack of sentimentality toward all things Ryerson ancestry. It was...un-pindown-able, Logan's attachment. Maybe it was Melba and their closeness. Maybe it was the fact that no one else in the family seemed to give an owl's hoot about the family's past. "I know, Mom. It's not that simple, though."

"Sure it is, hon. Ya don't have guests there. Put a CLOSED sign in the window and call a Realt'r. I think Devery Barnaby knows one. Or is she one? Oh, hon, I forget." She threw her voice off the phone and into the echo chamber that was their unadorned little home out in the 'burbs of the Twin City. "Norm! Is Devery Barnaby a real estate agent? Your second cousin. You know, Junie's daughter." A beat. "Okay, well would ya give me her phone number!" Another beat. "Just write it down, and I'll read it over the line! *Yes*, it's Logan. Yes, it's about the cottage, Norm!" A longer beat now, but Logan didn't dare interrupt. "Norm, you *said* to heck with that place, didn'tcha?

"Logan." His mother, likely fed up with Norm's

absent-mindedness, turned her attention back to the phone. "Hon, Dad's got Devery Barnaby's number right here. She's a cousin, 'member. I'll read it out to ya. Do you have a notepad and a pencil?"

"No, Mom. Can you text it?"

"I thought there wasn't a signal at the cottage, hon. Norm! Is there a cell phone signal there down at Melba's cottage, do ya know?"

"Mom, just give it to me." He held back an eye roll. "I'll give her a call if it comes to that."

"Comes to that? So yer not selling? Hon, now's the time, before you get tourists bangin' down that door."

"Well, Mom, I already have a couple of guests. They're here now." He lowered his voice and peered up the staircase, bracing for the emergence of either Kelly or Deb. The coast was clear, though. For now.

"Ya what? Since when? Golly, Logan, we were just in town. The funeral. Oh—is it the Berges? They were looking for a place en route to Mount Rushmore. 'Member, Norm? Melba's friend's kids, I think. Did ya talk to them at the funeral, Logan?"

"No, not the Berges, Mom."

"Oh."

He cleared his throat. "Just sightseers exploring the area." He hated to lie to his mother, but he didn't have a choice. Anyway, he could tell her everything in a month, once the cat was out of the bag. Heck, his mom would probably be calling him the first minute it was revealed that a real, live social media star was bunking up in Aunt Melba's old place. Anyway, Kelly and Deb were sort of sightseers, and they were exploring the area. At least, Deb had gone out that day. Though why Kelly hadn't joined her was hard to say.

"They're in the wrong area, I'd say! But that was always Melba's problem, wa'n't it, now, Norm? Wrong place, wrong time." Logan wasn't sure what that meant, and he was forgetting why he'd called his mother to begin with.

Oh, yeah. Advice. Well, he'd effectively gotten that. Sell the cottage. Only issue was he was stuck for the month. Couldn't exactly sell it out from under a TV star, or blogging star or whatever type of star Kelly was.

"So, what's up, buttercup?" his mom asked. He could practically hear her settle into the easy chair in the living room. A cup of milk at her elbow and a soap opera on TV. "Why'dya call? I mean don't get me wrong, I love to hear from my baby boy, but a mother's instinct and all. What's on yer mind, hon?"

She was right. There was a lot on his mind. Before Logan could piece together a response, his mom jumped in.

"It's Delilah, i'n't it?" Her voice was a little quieter now, and all background noise on her end was muted. His mother might be boisterous, but she was equally gentle.

Logan squeezed his eyes shut. Typically, with the very mention of that name, a sob would crawl up his throat.

But it didn't now. He opened his eyes again. "Actually, I don't think so."

"Oh?" This surprised his mother. Any time Logan had called her in the middle of the day for no other good reason, the real reason was Delilah. She knew it. He knew it. His dad knew it. Everyone knew it.

But no. This really wasn't about Delilah. It was about...Logan's next move. "You really think the cottage isn't worth keeping?"

"Oh, welp. That depends, hon."

"On what?"

"On the reason you're keeping it."

"You don't think Melba's legacy is enough?"

"Oh, no. I never said that. Melba's legacy is reason enough to fly to the moon and back. Doesn't mean you have to load yourself down with a dilapidated property, though. Take it from a Midwestern farmer's daughter, there's a lot to be said for modern conveniences. Look at your dad and me. Who'dda thought we'd be happy in a little condo? But, Logan, we don't have a lawn to cut or a coop to clean. Heck, hon, we hardly have to shovel snow. I'm telling you, Melba hated shoveling snow. She'd understand if you had to sell the thing. There are other ways to remember her."

"True." And it was.

"She'd want you to be happy. First and foremost. I knew Melba, and that woman had a heart the size of Jupiter, Logan. You do what makes you happy. That's how you honor ol' Aunt Melba."

ELIZABETH BROMKE

Logan mulled this over.

Eventually, his mother prompted him. "You don't have to keep the cottage, Logan. If coming back to Minneapolis and starting a new project for your business would make you happy, then that's what you do."

"What if keeping the cottage makes me happy?"

Chapter 18 — Kelly

A knock came at Kelly's door sometime after four in the afternoon. Kelly only registered it because she was starving. A hunger strike was not her style, but it was the only option in what was quickly becoming an austere situation.

She opened the door.

"Hi," Deb greeted her with an ashen look. "I have news."

"You do?"

Deb nodded. "Can I come in?"

They sat side by side on Kelly's bed, and everything —from Deb's tone to her body language to her refusal to meet Kelly's gaze—made it clear that the news was bad.

"Have you talked to Kyle?"

Deb chewed on her lower lip for some time. "Not exactly, but I got word about the closings on the two properties he was in charge of. They fell through."

"They did?" In the grand scheme of things, it didn't matter. Kelly had money to float her through to the next flip or the next TV spot. But in terms of what was currently going on with the business, this was bad.

"That's not all." Deb braved a glance in Kelly's direction then pulled up her phone, opening it to a bright white webpage with harsh red-and-black lettering.

Kelly's eyes flew across the headline. She didn't have to read it to take in the message, it was as though she'd known all along. After the moment's shock set in, she grabbed Deb's phone, to heck with the rules. She read aloud from Deb's screen. "BITCOIN BIGWIG KYLE FATALNY LEAVES HOMESTEAD FOR FOREIGN COUNTRY." The title was a weak attempt at a pun. Kelly scrolled down to see a paparazzi shot of Kyle with a woman who looked nothing like Kelly. Younger by at least ten years, maybe even twenty, and dark-haired with warm honey for skin to match her irises, the article called her Callistinia Montuguesa. She was a Brazilian model, apparently.

"Actually," Kelly said, handing the phone back to Deb, "this isn't a bad thing." She looked at her friend. "Right? I mean, *he* looks like the bad guy. Right?"

"And you the victim," Deb agreed tentatively. "Maybe." There was something else there. A weakness in Deb's expression. She was about to break. There was more to this barrage of bad news. A lot more?

"Deb. What is it." Kelly didn't ask. She demanded. She rarely demanded from Deb, but this required something more than a sugary-sweet request. "What's wrong?"

"The board wants a new direction now. They want me off the project."

"What?"

"Yeah. Um—" Deb squeezed her eyes shut, and her short black eyelashes were wet with tears. When Deb opened them again, her eyes were blurry. "They want a new direction. They don't want me to document your trip. They think it's too contrived. They say the stakes went up with all the drama back home, and no more playing Paris Hilton—going away to do the same ol' same ol' isn't gonna work, they say."

Kelly all but laughed. "What? This is ridiculous. They just want me to stay up here alone and then what? Go back home and do a documentary on what it was like to be in timeout for a month?" The laugh came, long and ridiculous and over-the-top. Logan had to hear her, but Kelly wanted him to. She wanted him to burst in and check on them or tear Kelly out of this nightmare and whisk her away for real. That's what she actually needed. A real man to whisk her away from her *contrived* life. Because actually, the board was right. All this? A joke. A play for follower sympathy and a way to climb back up the charts through grace and shame.

She came to her senses and passed the phone back to Deb. "This has to be a joke. Are you really going to leave me here, Deb?"

Deb only shrugged, and Kelly knew deep down that

when she established the board of supervisors, she was effectively passing off ownership of her own brand. She never imagined they'd turn on her to this degree.

"Deb, you can *stay*. Just don't document. Right?"

"If I stay, then what will the board do?"

"Deal with it, that's what. It's perfectly fine for me to have a travel partner here. A *friend* here. Right?" She was feeling hot and panicky now. "Right?"

But Deb, as sweet and motherly as she usually was, had only a cold response now. "The board doesn't see me that way and neither would viewers and followers."

"Then how in the world would they see you?"

"As your personal assistant." Deb was baleful now. "Nothing more. Nothing less." She dabbed a wadded up tissue at her face.

Kelly fell very still and spoke very evenly. "Why didn't the *board* think of this before?"

But Deb needn't have answered. Kelly knew the answer. Because *before*, at least Kelly still had a fiancé, and her fiancé was still back home hard at work on their flip projects. *Before*, Kelly had only been negligent and reckless, but she'd had other things, too. A passionate fanbase who wanted her to succeed.

Now, all she probably had was a sympathetic fanbase who questioned what was so wrong with Kelly Watts that she lost her brand, her fiancé, and any shred of hope that she might return to her business intact.

Now, all she had was a country cottage in South Dakota.

And the man who owned it.

May 6

W elp, there it is. Deb's leaving first thing in the morning. Meanwhile Logan's on a tear of some other kind. We haven't told him the news yet, so why is he acting like he's trying to save something?

Could it have anything to do with the other incident from this afternoon? Yeah. Get ready for full-on teenage goofiness here. This is something out of high school, and yet it felt as humiliating as this sort of thing would have been way back then.

Okay, so here we go. Oh wow. After Deb left my room, a huddle of burbling tears and fretting and hand wringing, I stepped into the hallway to use the bathroom. Not to go but to do the cliche thing that movie characters do after a hard moment: splash water on my face and pat it dry with a fluffy white towel. Of course, the towels here are a little more threadbare than fluff, but, you get the idea.

Anyway...

I go to open the door and—boom.

Logan.

No shirt.

A very threadbare *towel tied* very loosely *around his hips, sagging low on one side.*

He'd been leaning against the white porcelain pedestal sink, studying himself in the cherry-wood-trimmed oval mirror.

Oh sweet Lord, it was positively indecent. And what did I do? Did I quickly exit and close the door behind me and utter a quiet, mature apology?

Nope.

*I froze. As if I'd never seen a man in a towel before. Wait a minute...*have *I?*

I froze, and my eyes got stuck. Where? Oh, you know, on his butt. It felt like I stood there, staring, forever, which is ridiculous, because he looked up in the mirror and we locked eyes, and I couldn't even muster a single word. I just gaped at him and his butt and then at him again—as if his butt was separate from him as a person —until my trance broke. I have no idea what he was thinking, and I don't even know what he was doing *in there since he most definitely has a bathroom downstairs closer to the room where he stays. Just as soon as I came to, I fell backward and pulled the door with me, and then— THEN—it popped back open. The latch didn't catch, and it popped back open and sure enough there was Logan, now his hands securing the towel around his waist as he* twisted his torso and reached to push the door properly shut.

At last it was he who spoke first, through a straining, choking, cracking voice, mind you. "Sorry! I'm in here!" As if I didn't eventually come to realize just that.

Now I'm back in my room, still hot in the neck and face and still picturing every ripple in his back, from his spine cutting between two broad shoulders down to his hips, revealed just barely by that drooping, tattered rag-of-a-towel.

He's still in there. I can tell, because I haven't heard the door open and close again. In this place, you hear things like that. Not for lack of white noise—there's plenty, from the cooler that kicks on after a running start down to the braying goats from out back. But you hear things like that in this little place because that's how old farmhouses and cottages are. They're more like people. They talk. And they breathe. In and out.

In and out.

In and out.

Chapter 19 — Logan

He didn't want to leave the bathroom. Not after that. His own shower was on the fritz, but he was trying hard to make tonight's dinner extra special. That meant a shower and shave, then a smorgasbord of comfort food.

Here he was, though, still in the bathroom. His hand still held over a racing heart.

Logan hadn't realized the lock didn't work on the bathroom door. He hadn't realized the latch sometimes didn't catch. This was one of two upstairs baths, and he just hadn't put time into learning about the quirks of the place yet. Now, he knew. Thank goodness, however, it hadn't been the other way around. What might have happened if he'd walked in on Kelly?

For a fleeting moment, he let his mind go there. He let himself indulge in the idea of seeing another woman in something other than her clothes. In a flimsy towel. A robe. *Anything*.

It felt good. Not the fantasy. He wasn't a total degenerate. What felt good was letting himself think about other women. In *that* way. That enchantment of what-ifs and daydreams and the blushing side of his imagination. It was probably healthy. Had to be healthy. There, it was. It was healthy for Logan to think about Kelly Watts as a sensual woman in nothing more than a slinky towel wrapped around her glistening, fresh-from-the-shower body just in time for Logan to accidentally open the door and—

What was *wrong* with him! He was a total degenerate. What if she thought he didn't lock the door on purpose, even? What if she hadn't yet realized the door didn't lock and she thought he was some sort of a Midwestern perv!

Oh, geez. This was bad. Really bad. How long could he sweat it out? The door didn't lock after all, so it couldn't be long. Next, he'd be covering his manhood in time for Deb to barge in.

Oh, *geez*!

He splashed cold water on his face to cool off and calm the heck down. Be cool. She walked in on *you*. This was *not* your fault. Move forward. Big dinner. Show the guests a great visit. Make everything go smoothly. You'll get great reviews. Things'll take off. You can stay on here, happily. You'll never have to go back to Minneapolis again except when you want to.

You don't have to live there. Work there. This is a new beginning.

Just move *forward*.

He swallowed and studied himself in the mirror. Logan looked a little leaner than usual. This had been a battle for the past two years. Eating enough. A battle he'd never have predicted for himself. Growing up on mashed potatoes and steak, baked beans and casseroles, it was easy enough to put meat on his bones. But these last two were hard. He could turn it around, though. It was all about your mindset. He knew this.

He grabbed his clean shirt from the hook on the back of the door and tugged it on. It was a blue cotton button-down. He'd packed it as a back-up for the funeral, actually. Then the jeans. Then the boots. Logan only ever wore boots, important occasion or otherwise. He'd return to his own bathroom to fix his hair and spritz on cologne, if he could find some. Uncle Norm Senior had to have some, somewhere. What Prairie Creek man didn't keep a bottle of Prairie Wind in his medicine cabinet? Then again, did Uncle Norm die before that brand of fragrances had come out? Who knew? Not Logan.

Satisfied that he was fully clothed and ready to leave the bathroom and venture down the common hall toward the staircase, Logan pulled the door open a crack to peek out first. The coast was clear. He glanced behind him and grabbed his now-infamous towel and turned back, stepping through the door and smack into Kelly.

Their collision would have been comical if not for

the recent other foible. His hands broke the crash, landing along her arm, but she pivoted toward him as their bodies met, and one of his hands wound up awkwardly on her stomach. He pulled back as fast as he could. "I am so sorry. Wow. I'm just—clumsy today or something."

"You're clumsy? I think I'm the one who's goofing up today. Well, every day, lately."

"That's the point of life, right?" He stepped back and smoothed his shirt and ran his fingers through his wet hair. "To goof up?"

Kelly didn't smile though. "I thought the point was to *not* goof up."

"Where's the fun in that?" They were still close to each other. Maybe just inches apart. If Logan wasn't imagining it, Kelly's face swayed in toward his.

His chest tightened. Her eyes fixed on his. She said, "I don't remember the last time I had fun because of a goof-up."

Then, it was as though space and time and fate convened in that very moment. It was as though Logan knew the next move. And, he had to take it. Despite their circumstances (she was his guest) and his past (Delilah was slowly drifting further into the recesses of his heart and mind).

Logan ran his tongue over his lips and closed the narrow gap between them, effectively taking back the step he'd made after bumping into her. "I can help with that, you know," he whispered.

"Help with what?" she asked.

He stared at her mouth, the pretty shape of it. Her pale, freckled face with subtle laugh lines at the corners of her eyes. Somewhere in her life she'd had fun. Maybe not lately, though.

Then it hit him. She was engaged. The shock of the realization jolted him backward, but by then, Kelly was obviously thinking the same thing—*doing* the same thing. Her eyes had been falling closed, her lips closer to his face than the rest of her body.

"You're engaged," he murmured, bracing his hands against her shoulders. "I'm sorry—I was—"

"Goofing up?" She didn't look embarrassed or let down or anything. She looked...amused.

He smiled, but it was a sad one, because the reality was he'd been impatient. He'd developed a fast crush on this woman, and he'd almost acted on it. And come to think of it, maybe the only reason Logan wanted to stay at the cottage was the minuscule hope that he would woo her or something.

But her soft look persisted, and Kelly added, "Actually, I'm not engaged. Not anymore. That was over, we were just—it wasn't an authentic relationship. I mean—" She stopped short, her eyebrows knitting together. "It's complicated."

He nodded. He understood complicated. "Want to talk about it?"

"Actually?" She brightened. "Yes."

Chapter 20 — Kelly

Kelly joined Logan in the kitchen, where she offered to help him with supper. It was her forte, after all.

And if they were cooking, she felt like she could really let go and vent. Not that she ought to be venting, but if she was about to lose the only friend she had and if her board was so disgusted that they were cutting the cord, well, it was time Kelly found other ways to survive.

Anyway, since the moment she'd seen Logan on the tarmac, she was taken. And as Kelly reflected about *why* she was taken, she knew there was more to the attraction than Logan's good looks. Good looks were plentiful. Even in her industry, at conferences and meet-and-greets and signings, she'd shaken hands with movie stars and models. Her inbox was swamped with propositions and proposals from twenty-something Lotharios with great hair, icy blue eyes, and a tan too perfect for this world.

So why Logan Ryerson? South Dakota Logan with his aunt's little cottage inn and a mysterious backstory? What did Kelly even know about this guy?

Well, she knew he was a family guy. He loved his aunt. She knew he was a small-town boy, like her. She knew he was polite to women and helpful but not pushy. She knew what her gut told her, frankly. And if there was one thing Kelly's mother had taught her—beyond the cooking and cleaning and decorating—it was to trust your instinct. Implicitly. You're walking along the road and feel someone's presence uncomfortably behind you? Slip into the nearest gas station. Wait him out. You call up an electrician to upgrade your panel and he comes across a little slimy? Go with someone else.

You meet a handsome guy with a fat savings account, great car, all the charm in the world but *something's not right*?

Leave him.

Unfortunately for Kelly, she hadn't followed her instinct on Kyle. But now it didn't matter. Kyle was old news. And so was the life Kelly thought she had built.

But the funny thing was, Kelly's instinct told her that wasn't such a bad thing.

"Okay, fried pork chops, buttery mashed potatoes, Brussels sprouts, and dessert depends on the season. Apple pie, pumpkin pie, pecan pie, or lemon merengue." Kelly looked over the handwritten page Logan had passed to her. It was a course meal of Aunt Melba's, which the woman had even given a name to: *The Country*

Cottage Special. "This is the sweetest thing I've ever seen. She calls it *The Country Cottage Special*, did she call this place the country cottage, too?"

"It was always just Ryersons', since it opened to the public. I don't think that was because anyone named the place Ryersons'. Rather, I think people knew Ned and Melba Ryerson lived here, and so that's what they called it. The Ryersons'."

"Will you keep it that name, too?"

Logan set about pulling ingredients out of cupboards and the fridge, setting everything out on the kitchen island, a butcher block slab just the right height for all things food prep.

Kelly couldn't help but imagine herself rolling out sugar cookie dough on a spray of flour here and guiding a little girl's hands over cookie cutters at Christmas time, with snow falling outside like in some enchanting holiday movie. She zapped the image from her brain and tried to focus. Get through this month. Get back to Texas. Rebuild the public's trust in her. Rebuild her brand. Reclaim the life she worked so hard to build.

Logan answered her question. "I suppose. It's how people know the place."

Kelly couldn't help but wonder if people really did know the place, though. It was so out of the way and so—

Wait a minute. "Is that how Deb found you? And my board of supervisors?"

"Pardon?" Logan asked.

She didn't mean to accuse him, but there was no way Logan was exempt from the drama. He had to be in on it.

But for her to press him on the matter would mean she'd reveal why exactly she was here. What she had to do with Joanna Hayfield.

"Did they find you by doing a deep dive into Joanna Hayfield's past? They obviously tracked down her family, which wasn't hard to do. But from there, did they just look for the closest motel to her hometown or does your family have deeper ties to the Hayfields?"

Logan looked more confused than ever, a package of raw, pink pork chops suspended in his hand in midair. "Sorry?"

The answer came from behind them. Deb. "He had nothing to do with it, Kelly."

Kelly turned to face her *assistant*. "How can you be sure? Was it even you who found this place?"

"You can put your defenses down. No one wants to see you fail."

"No, they just want to see me suffer." Kelly hated her own attitude, but she couldn't seem to stop the onslaught of negative emotions flooding her body. Even in the midst of what was set to be a perfect night. After an almost-kiss with Logan and their plan here to make dinner together. She shouldn't be this angry. But she was. She was very, very angry.

"Listen," Logan chimed in, "I don't know anything about what you do, but I know a thing or two about business. And, I don't want to involve myself unnecessarily, but whatever it is you're mad about, I mean regarding your directors or whatever, it's not about you. It's about your business. Their business is your business, right?"

"I've always hated that, though. The idea that *it's not personal, it's business.* Of course it's personal. I made this business. The business is based on my life. On my home and all that I do in my home and all that I do for other people's homes."

Logan looked helpless and rested the meat on a waiting plate. "I guess it'd help if you'd clue me in on what it is you do. And why you're not engaged. And why you're here."

His tone wasn't harsh, but it wasn't gentle, either. Kelly realized that Logan wasn't just a prop in her project anymore. He was all she'd have left come tomorrow morning. And the almost-kiss. What about it? Where was this going? Where did she want it to go? What did she want him to know and not know?

And most of all, did she want to keep things from the one person she'd be relying on for nearly a month?

"Okay, here's what happened."

April 30

Homestead and Hearth: Official Media Release
It is with sadness in hearts that we report
the passing of *H&H* client, Mrs. Joanna
Hayfield. For those who follow us, you may recognize her
from a recent home flipping project in Dallas. In our
experience with Mrs. Hayfield, we came to know her as a
sharp lady with fine tastes in home decor. She was a treasured client, to be sure. It is with the family's permission
that we share the tragic details.

To be very clear on the events that unfolded, it is
important we share with our followers the chain of
events. While we at *H&H* take every opportunity to
secure highly qualified and competent professionals in
every step of our home renovation projects, we cannot
always foresee problems.

Unfortunately, with the home Mrs. Hayfield
purchased for renovation, there were structural issues,

particularly concerning the front stoop, where evident rotting persisted. Despite our best efforts to rectify the issues by first warning Mrs. Hayfield against entering the property via the front entry, egress was attempted. Mrs. Hayfield suffered a fall. While precautions were taken to avoid any injury, we were unable to effectively prevent this incident. Mrs. Hayfield succumbed to her injuries and complications from the fall last night.

Thanks to *H&H*'s insurance policy, we are able to provide substantially to the family in compensation. Of course, financial compensation is never enough, as we at *H&H* genuinely believe that human life is priceless. It is here and now that we wish to submit our sincerest apologies to the Hayfield and Barnaby families for their suffering, and we pray for Mrs. Hayfield on her journey into Heaven. God has gained an angel, but Earth as well as her family has lost their beloved Joanna. May you rest in peace.

As a small aside, many have written in and called asking about additional consequences to the company and our "star," Kelly Watts. In time, Kelly will make her own statement on the tragedy. For now, she is on an unpaid, extended leave of absence from *H&H*. Though Kelly's own actions did not explicitly result in Mrs. Hayfield's death, she takes very seriously the matters of liability and responsibility and feels earnestly that she can do better and will do better.

With sincerest condolences,
All of us at Homestead and Hearth

Chapter 21 — Logan

L ogan took in Kelly's story as they steadily worked together on supper. Deb set the table, piping up only when necessary, to remind everybody that the whole thing was a sad tragedy, but it was an *accident*.

Kelly whipped a batter with which to coat the chops while Logan boiled potatoes and seasoned the cast iron in the meantime.

"I guess I don't understand," he said once it was time to mash the potatoes and pull the pork chops from their sizzling oil.

Kelly popped open the fridge, a white, early model Frigidaire complete with the silver handle that you had to tug hard on in order to free up the vacuum seal. She was fairly certain these things were outlawed or something, due to kids getting stuck inside. It turned out to be more of an icebox than a fridge, and the butter she needed showed signs of freezer burn.

Logan must have read her mind. "Here." He passed her a fresh stick of butter, room-temperature and soft.

"Thanks. But," she referred back to his remark. "What's not to understand?" Kelly asked.

"Joanna's fall wasn't your fault. You told Mrs. Haymaker—I mean Hayfield—not to enter through the front door. She did it anyway."

"My contractor should have put up caution tape or sawhorses to keep her from going there."

"Actually, Kyle was the project manager. He should have."

"He wasn't the contractor," Kelly argued.

"Who's Kyle?" Logan asked.

Both women looked at him.

"That's the complicated part I was telling you about," Kelly replied with a shudder. She plated the pork chops and started rummaging through the fridge again.

"What are you looking for now?" Logan asked.

Her head reemerged from the crisper bins. "Garnish?"

"Such as?"

"Apple sauce or herbs? Even sprigs of rosemary?"

Logan looked again at Melba's instructions. "No garnish."

Kelly seemed surprised. "Well, you always want to add a little pop."

"There's no garnish on the *Country Cottage Special,* though." He held it up. "See?"

"Well, sure, but—" then she shook her head. "You're right. Melba knew what she was doing."

He pulled the Brussels sprouts from the oven and Kelly scooped the potatoes onto plates, and soon enough they were seated at the dining room table, plates chock full of a meal any Midwesterner would be proud of.

"This is awkward, but I'm used to saying Grace."

"So am I," Kelly replied.

Deb smiled. "It's my last night here. I'll start." Before Logan could protest or inquire about what she meant, she took off, head bowed, hands clasped. "O Heavenly Father, thank You for this chance to support Kelly and to know Mr. Logan Ryerson. He's a real sweetheart and a treasure. And I know he's fit to take care of Kelly in this troublin' time in her life. But above all that, I know that You are fit to take care of us all under Your watchful blessed eye. In Christ's name we pray. Amen."

"Amen," Kelly and Logan recited together.

Logan looked up. "You're leaving?" Then he looked at Kelly. "And you're—*staying*?" If he had this right, it meant that he and Kelly would have the cottage to themselves. It was a little much. A lot much, maybe. But then, so was the cottage. So was Melba's death and Logan's past and all the emotions swirling around in his heart and in his head.

Kelly and Deb exchanged a look. "It's back to the complicated part."

"What is so complicated?" he asked.

Kelly cut into her meat. "Shall we?" She pointed to it with her fork, then stabbed it and lifted it to smell. "This is going to be divine." She didn't wait for the others, and Logan couldn't help but watch as she parted her lips and slipped the crispy, golden cut into her mouth, chewing slowly, pruriently.

He cleared his throat.

Deb was shoveling through the potatoes, all but checked out of the conversation entirely.

Kelly finally replied, but only after dabbing her lips with her napkin. "Kyle was my fiancé. He's a Bitcoin investor, among other things. We dated seriously, then he proposed, but it was a little bit put-on by the board. Anyway, after the engagement, they wanted Kyle to join the brand in a more prominent role. They felt like I needed a partner. A lot of other influencers have partners."

Deb spoke with her mouth full. "Think of Chip and Joanna Gaines."

Logan swallowed a scrumptiously savory morsel of pork chop. It reminded him of his mom and dad and Christmas time. And Aunt Melba. It reminded him of home to eat this food. He'd been subsisting too much on junk as of late. "Chip and Joanna who?" he asked.

"Never mind that. The point was, Kyle was never cut out for renovating or decorating or flipping houses."

"But he joined you anyway?"

"He's fame hungry and greedy."

"And you were engaged to this guy?"

"Remember? It was sort of a ploy for followers?" Kelly winced.

Logan was surprised that she'd go along with such a ploy, but then—he didn't know her. All he knew was she was a celebrity who he did not know, which probably spoke volumes in and of itself. He tried to quell the unease that developed in his chest.

Kelly must have read him, though, because she promised, "It's not my style. None of what has happened is my style, Logan. I swear. I know words don't mean much, and I try to set an example through my actions, but this whole thing has gotten out of control. And it began with bringing Kyle in. He took over this flip project. It was a dilapidated rehab situation this little old lady had purchased. She was a devout fan, I guess, and one of her friends put her name in to win a home and a reno. She won. She came down to Dallas, and she hadn't made any other plans. We offered to put her in a hotel, which is usual anyway. She refused. She said she didn't stay in hotels. They made her itch." Kelly's mouth twitched with amusement.

Logan outright laughed. "That sounds like ol' Mrs. Haymaker."

"Anyway, she insisted on staying *in* the home she'd won. We cautioned her against it. Then another project came up that was supposed to be my prime piece. Kyle was to take over on the Hayfield House, as we called it.

He was supposed to expedite things and get her in there safely."

"But he didn't," Logan guessed.

"Right."

"And she fell and died," Deb added, unnecessarily.

Kelly glanced Deb's way. "Yeah."

"And they blamed this on you? It wasn't your fault. I know Mrs. Haymaker. You couldn't change her mind if you had a million dollars. Once it's set, it's set. If she wanted to go and sleep in someone's ramshackle hut, she was going to do it. And if she was going to walk up rotted-out steps, well, she was going to do it."

"It was my project, though. I should have had an easier access point for her. I should have had tape up. There were a million things I could have and should have done and didn't."

"But it was Kyle's project."

"That's just it though," Deb interjected through mouthfuls of fried pork. "Kelly knew that Kyle was useless."

Kelly and Logan both stared at Deb in disbelief. Logan's disbelief was in Deb's boldness and in Kelly's low standards. He wasn't sure why Kelly was shocked to hear what the woman said.

"Why were you with him, again?" Logan couldn't help it. He felt a sense of ownership and protectiveness over Kelly, even though he'd known her for such a minimal amount of time. There it was, that bonding feeling he couldn't shake. The attraction. The interest. The *pull*.

"The point is, I'm not anymore. He dropped the ball, and I recognize that. And I'm repenting for whatever fault I had. That's why I'm here."

"And you're here to win your followers back," Deb pointed out by way of pointing her fork at Kelly.

Logan held up a hand and wiped his mouth with the other before asking, "So the company sent you away to find yourself. But I don't get it. Why would they send you to Joanna's hometown? It can't be coincidence."

"It's not," Deb answered for Kelly. "It's the board's way of setting up for a big reveal."

"A big reveal of what?" he asked.

Kelly looked embarrassed. She fell entirely quiet and stared at her plate.

Deb answered him. "Every reality show or influencer has big reveals. Things that come at the end of a season or the end of a series or the end of a segment either. Sometimes it's a cliffhanger. Sometimes it's a Come-to-Jesus."

Everything was falling together. He saw the picture clearly now. Kelly wasn't sent to his cottage to live in nature and work the land. She was there to apologize to the Hayfields in person and earn their green light to move forward with another renovation somewhere down the line. It was all for publicity.

It was all a stunt.

He folded his napkin, set his jaw, and pushed back from the table. "I see."

"Logan, wait." Kelly was reaching for him, but he was up and out of his seat and moving toward the kitchen to clean up. "You didn't want to experience Ryersons' or a country cottage. You wanted to appease the masses. I get it."

He didn't wait for her to explain or make excuses. He tuned her out as she was trying to convince him that none of this was her idea, she was only doing her job.

And that's when he realized that the thing he thought could make him happy, living there at the cottage and hosting guests like some little innkeeping grandmother—it was a stunt, too.

Maybe Kelly and her *brand* weren't the only frauds in Prairie Creek. Maybe Logan was a fraud too.

Chapter 22 — Kelly

"Great." Kelly's appetite had left with Logan. She looked at Deb. "Just great. He thinks I'm a joke, too."

"You've still got me," Deb reasoned.

"You're leaving too," Kelly reminded her. "And anyway, you're not my friend. Just my assistant. Right?"

Deb wadded her napkin and dropped it on the table next to her plate. "You know what, Kelly Watts? I'm not going to be your assistant for another second, I'm going to be your friend."

"Good! I need a friend!" Kelly was on the verge of tears, but she was doing everything in her power to salvage her dignity in the face of this total humiliation and ruin.

"Okay, as your *friend*, I'm done." Deb's face was different than Kelly had ever seen it before.

But that didn't discourage Kelly from fighting back. After all, all she had left in her life was the fight inside of her. The fight to live on after her mom died. The fight to make money doing something she loved. The fight to remain successful in spite of tragedy. "You're done as my assistant, so what else is new?"

"No. I'm not done *being* your friend. I'm done playing into your pity party, Kelly. You've got it made. You've got a great, *growing* business with a team behind you. Other people manage it, so you don't have to. Other people schedule things for you. All you have to do is pick out wallpaper and post it online. Your life is good. So you know what? I think this'll do you good."

Deb stood and pushed her chair in. "It's time for you to realize that the world hasn't stopped just because they have a bone to pick with a social media star. Did you know this whole scandal has *increased* your popularity? Did you know that when Joanna Hayfield's death became news, you gained four-hundred *thousand* new followers? On *each* platform? Did you know you're profiting from that woman's death?"

Kelly's face burned as if both cheeks had been slapped. She couldn't make eye contact with Deb. It was all she could do not to melt into a puddle on the floor. But if she did that, then she was exactly what Deb had called her. A human self-pity party who just happened to profit off of the death of a poor old woman.

Deb started to leave, but before she was gone, Kelly whispered, "How do I fix it?"

Deb stopped and rested a hand on Kelly's shoulder. "The same way you fix a house. From the inside out."

May 10

I t's been several days since Deb left and over a week since I've been here. The past few days have been different than the first few, though.

After Deb left, Logan tried to play hotelier. He cleaned and fixed stuff. The first of which was the bathroom lock. The second of which was his own shower on the first floor.

I used that day to recover and write. I wrote pages and pages, and I've ripped them all out, because not a single entry went anywhere. I would start one, and soon enough it derailed into feeling sorry for myself. Sorry my mom died and that my dad fell out of the picture of my life. Sorry for myself that I don't have a normal job—hah! Sorry for myself about Joanna's death and Kyle's affair and Deb's leaving me. I needed that though. I need to vent to some-one, somehow.

The next day, I took to the farm. I walked and walked,

every square inch, and there are acres of them. Acres upon acres. I met the goats and fed them. I came across a family of deer. I think I even saw the locally and globally fabled pheasants when I came to a little meadow out past the creek that runs through the farm. Logan told me later that the creek is actually Prairie Creek, and that made me think a little differently of this place.

So the next day, I asked Logan to sit down with me and tell me more about Aunt Melba and Uncle Ned and the original Ryersons. I asked him to tell me everything he could about Prairie Creek.

He tried, but in the end, he said there was only one way to learn about this small town he once called home.

So today, we're going into town together. In the truck. Alone. Other than the comfort-food meals he continues to make for breakfast, lunch, and dinner, this will be our first real alone time together. And, it's an excursion. I hope he'll forgive me for being horrible and for what my company stands for. But I also know that words can't bring about forgiveness.

Only actions can.

Of course, the action I have in mind is pretty grand. It might even have consequences of its own.

Scratch that. I know *for a fact it* has *consequences. If I follow through on this, Diary, it could mean the end of everything.*

But it could mean the beginning, too.

Sometimes, to really fix something, you have to start

over. So, here I go, tearing down walls and looking deep down into the basement of my soul to fix this house from within. To fix me. Who knows? Maybe I'll finally have the dream home I've always been searching for. Even better? Maybe someone else will want to share it with me this time.

Chapter 23 — Logan

Logan's heart had softened in the days since Deb had left. Maybe because it was just him and Kelly in the cottage or maybe because of a greater force. Maybe it's who he was.

Today he planned to show Kelly around town and give her an idea of where it was she was stuck. Where Joanna Hayfield came from. Where he'd come from, too. Anyway, he needed a break from oiling squeaky hinges and patching nail holes. He needed to be reminded, too, why he was in Prairie Creek, the hometown he'd once left for greener pastures.

They were in the truck, and his hands were clammy as all get out. He ran each down his thighs and started the ignition before casting a glance at Kelly. She was gussied up a bit, in a pretty pink sundress with those tan-colored sandals that had a lot of straps zigzagging. On her face she wore oversize sunglasses. Her hair was down, in the same wild curls he recalled from their first day together. But she had a beige hair tie on her wrist, like she was ready for business. It reminded him that he still couldn't be sure who Kelly Watts was. A real person? Freckle-faced and soft-skinned and lovely? Or an avatar? A persona for screen-time addicts?

"Don't forget to buckle up," he chided, but she was already strapped in and beaming back at him. Satisfied and maybe a hint giddy, he started the engine.

For the first while of their drive, along the dirt drive and the dirt road that would carry them to the highway, they were both quiet. Kelly kept her eyes out the passenger window.

Flowers bloomed along the roadside in bright oranges and whites, and Logan wished he could point to them and tell her what they were, but he never had been very good at horticulture. Instead, he let her think, and he thought, too. Mostly, about what to say. Or ask.

At last, a question came to mind. "So, while you're here, are you taking notes? Think you'll come back with a camera to get more footage down the road or something? I'd hate for you to waste the time you've spent here."

"Waste it?" She looked at him and frowned. "How could it be wasted?"

"Well, wasn't the point to document your *recovery*, of sorts?"

"At first, yeah. That's over now, though."

He squinted at the roadsigns ahead as though he

didn't have them committed to memory long since. "Here's our exit."

"This is Prairie Creek?" She leaned forward and looked closer as he slowed the car and veered off left, taking a frontage road onto Main Street.

"Yep."

They rolled past Church Street Cemetery on the right. He pointed to the chapel beyond it. "That's where I went to church. First Faith Presbyterian."

"I'm Presbyterian, too," she commented.

A little ways down, they crossed Schoolhouse Lane, but not before he pointed left and said, "There's the grade school and down farther is the secondary school. I went to both, of course."

"What's their mascot?"

"I'll give you three guesses, but you'll only need one."

"Prairie dog?" she tried.

"Nope."

"Bison?"

"Wrong again."

"Oh, of course. Has to be. The pheasant."

He grinned. "Bingo."

Soon enough they were in the thick of downtown Prairie Creek, which, truth be told, was as much of a downtown as Austin is a quiet suburb.

"There's the café you talked about." She pointed to Maisie's. "And that's the bakery. There's the little pet shop, so cute. Oh, is this the hardware store you come to?"

Logan didn't have to look out her window to nod. "Yep."

"What's that one, there?"

He followed her finger to a more prominent building that popped out from the southern strip of storefronts. "That was my grandmother's crafting place."

"Laundry, Vac, and Sew," Kelly read.

"My granddad on my mom's side was a vacuum repairman. He kept a few washing machines and dryers in there, too. Later on, I guess. He was into logging, too. He sort of did a little bit of everything. And his wife, my Grandma Betty, was a seamstress."

"Wow," she breathed. "It's adorable. Is it closed now?"

"Yes and no. My grandad owns it and lives there, but the business shuttered once my grandma passed a coupla years ago."

"I'm so sorry."

"I appreciate it. It was...the hardest time of my life." He was surprised to hear himself say it. Everyone who already knew Logan knew that year was his worst. Miles knew it, and it was why Miles kept popping in on him from time to time over the last few days. His mom and dad knew it, which was why they followed him to Minneapolis to begin with. Sigh. Logan knew it worst of all. But was he really ready to share that with Kelly? Would she understand? She couldn't know a pain like that. Not when she lived a life so different. An artificial one.

Still, he couldn't help but wonder if he was starting to see the real Kelly. The layers that existed beneath the screen.

"You were close to her?"

He jolted from her question and pulled to a stop at the roundabout that would take them around the traffic circle that encompassed town hall. "Close to her? Of course I was." What kind of a question was that?

But clarity came when Kelly added, "I was never close to my grandparents. They lived in another city, and my parents didn't like to travel." She gave a short laugh. "I guess my grandparents didn't like to, either, because they never came to visit us. I always regretted that I couldn't get to know them more. I think that's why I like to work on old houses. It's one way for me to learn about a past that was sort of... kept me from as a girl." She shook her head. "That's silly, I know."

It wasn't silly at all, but now Logan felt that way for thinking Kelly was asking about Delilah. "I wasn't that close to Grandma Betty. Not like my sister was. I actually meant I was close to, um, my wife. Delilah."

Chapter 24 — Kelly

"Wife? You're married?" It was ridiculous for Kelly to feel an instant pang of envy, but there it was. Her blood felt hot in her veins as it rushed into her neck. A fool to try to kiss him. And justified in laying low the last few days. "I didn't realize."

Then she whipped to face him. "But you tried to kiss me." She said this aloud even as it occurred to her. Their intimate moment in the hall—their glances at each other —cooking together—all of it made no sense if he was married.

She looked at his left hand hanging loosely on the steering wheel. No ring.

"She died," he said, calmly, his eyes straight ahead as he pulled around the traffic circle and into a parking spot among a row of empty ones in front of a little grassy knoll. They sat there together, quietly.

After several moments, Kelly said, "I'm so sorry. I can't imagine."

Without further prompting, Logan explained. "My sister, Mabel, Grandma Betty, and my wife, Delilah, were all driving together in Mabel's car. It was winter. There was snow and ice on the ground. My sister wasn't paying attention. They were traveling from the shop there—" he jutted his chin toward the little store-front that stood out yet along the bank of others. "They were heading to my parents' house for a Sunday dinner. It wasn't a holiday or anything. Just a Sunday dinner. Grandpa Kimble, that's my mom's maiden name, Kimble, didn't come. He never leaves the upstairs of that place. It's like he's trapped. He stayed. Grandma Betty got in the car with Mabel and Delilah. I was at my parents' house. Just waiting for the girls to pick her up. It was just a nice thing for them that day. Girl bonding time or something. I was helping my mom with supper.

"We didn't have to wait for the police to show up to know something had happened. They should have been back within an hour. Once two hours had passed with no word, we called Grandpa Kimble. He said they'd left a long while ago. I got in my truck and drove the way there, keeping my eye out. It was dark, but I spotted it. The white-yellow car just over the ditch and stuck in rows of a roadside shelter belt. Bushes or trees of some kind. I had never noticed before. We've got those things—the shelter belts—everywhere."

Kelly's eyes stung and her mouth gaped at him. She was enraptured and aching for Logan. For his family.

He didn't look at her but instead pressed on with the story after a deep sigh. "I pulled over, didn't bother to call 9-1-1. I ran across the ditch, slipping all over the dang place, getting stuck in waist-deep snow until I made it to the other side. I pulled myself up like a mountain climber. I moved fast, faster than ever before in my life. I pushed through the stalks of corn, I think it had to have been corn. I got to the driver's side first. I'll never forget that, either. I knew that Delilah was in the backseat. She was just that way. She'd have let Grandma Betty ride shotgun." He laughed a little, and Kelly's heart warmed over a touch.

"Mabel was out of it. I mean totally unconscious. I thought she was dead, but she had a pulse. I left her there and went to Grandma Betty next. I reached over my sister, and hit the overhead lights. When they came on, I saw all I needed to see. Both my grandmother and my wife were gone. I took it for granted that Delilah would be fine. In my mind, she was young and tough and full of life, like Mabel." He stole a look at Kelly. "You know Delilah was a housewife? It was her life's goal. I always thought she deserved more than that. I always thought she could have the world. She could do anything, but she didn't want it. She just wanted to sit at home and watch reality TV and paint her toenails, I think. That's what it meant to her. But I loved her anyway. I'd come home and she'd talk about her TV drama. She'd have loved you, I'm sure. She'd know who you are."

Kelly felt embarrassed at that, but she offered him a small smile of encouragement. "She sounds lovely. Sweet."

"She was. By the time I got back there to her, I realized she was worse off than Mabel and Grandma." He shook his head and a look of disappointment crossed his features. "She hadn't worn her seatbelt." Then, his face whipped to her. "I don't mean she deserved to die, but it was hard not to be mad."

"It wasn't her fault, but I get it. I'd be mad, too. Like I was at my mom, kind of."

"Your mom?"

"She had cancer. Refused chemo. Said that God had chosen her. That her time was up. I tried to tell her that God also offered her chemo, but—she was too stubborn." Kelly swallowed hard. Then, she felt something tickle her fingertips on the seat between them. She looked down to see Logan's hand edging itself to her, brushing her fingers. She lifted her palm and his hand slid under hers. Their fingers interlocked.

Kelly let her tears spill down her cheeks. She hadn't cried about her mom in a long time, but maybe these tears were for more than just her grief over her mother's passing. Maybe they were tears for her career. Her failed would-be engagement. Her loss of friendship or the fact that she'd never spent the time to make new friends. Being a career woman in the social sphere was a little too cutthroat for that, and it was a sad thing to think about now that Kelly had the time and space to think about it. There was much, much more to be sad about.

But, there was something to be happy about too. "Can I tell you something?" she said after he'd let her cry, squeezing her hand every half a moment and finally pulling her into him. They were two broken people, sitting in his blue truck in the center of Prairie Creek like a couple of old pals. It was time to tell Logan.

"Of course," he said.

"I'm not going back."

He scooted half an inch away and looked at her. "What?"

Kelly locked eyes with Logan and repeated, "I'm not going back.

"To Texas?"

"To *Homestead and Hearth*."

"What about to Texas? Are you going back there?" His stare was intense, focused, imploring. It was as though these two strangers, who'd been thrust together under conditions outside of their control, were of the same mind. Cut from the same cloth. Conjoined some-how, by the fates, maybe. Or just, plain luck.

"I don't know," she answered, her voice wobbly. "I mean. Not yet." She ran her tongue over her lips. "Unless you want me to go back soon? I guess there's no point in me being here now."

"Did you tell them? Your board or whatever? Deb? How'd she take it?"

He spoke about the people in Kelly's life like he knew them. That's what happened, she guessed, when you were in close quarters with someone. Your lives intertwined seamlessly. "Deb was encouraging. She said we could be friends now."

"You're really leaving your business? Like, *for good*?" He was slack jawed. "But, how can it go on?"

"The brand can go on, and it will. They've already got an up-and-coming influencer champing at the bit to take my place. There are probably fifty more. I think the mark of a good brand is that it doesn't hinge on any one person. I guess I was successful in that way." Sadness swelled back up in her chest. "But it means I'm free to go. The board can grant me that. They'll vote to release me from the contract. And technically, I'm on contract through the summer. Which means, *technically*, I have to stay here until the month is up." She looked at him, pleading. "If you'll have me?"

He squeezed her hand. "You can stay as long as you'd like, Kelly. I mean that."

"Even after—" she didn't have to finish her sentence. The conversation of dinner days back was old news now. It was as though it was a necessary evil. They were past it. They'd moved on.

"I'm looking for a little help, you know," he said.

"Help? At the cottage?" She couldn't help that a little grin formed on her mouth. "With what?"

"Well, with marketing for starters." He put the truck in drive. "After all, I have my first guests—real ones—

coming this weekend. A couple of RVers on their way to Mount Rushmore."

"Guests, huh?" she was impressed. "So other people are looking to leave technology behind and rough it under a quilt for a vacation? Or, wait, don't tell me—they have to make a public apology to a family whose grandparent died on their time, too?" Her smile fell off, and her stomach roiled in guilt and sadness all over again.

Logan grimaced. "You don't have to do that, Kelly. Especially if the jig is up, you know."

"I'm going to do it. I'm here. I just need to find them. Now that I don't have the resources I did before, it'll be more sincere. More pathetic, anyway."

"It's not pathetic. It's good of you. But it's unnecessary." He cleared his throat. "I sometimes wish I could go back and do things over, too, ya know."

"Really?"

"Who doesn't? But Kelly, that's part of life, right?"

She looked at him, and a smile crackled over her own face to match his. "Goofing up, you mean?"

Instead of answering her, Logan put the truck back in park, and right there, in the heart of Prairie Creek, in the little blue pickup truck, with Logan in his red flannel shirt and jeans and Kelly in her pink sundress and espadrilles, Logan hooked his hands around her head, pulled Kelly in, and *kissed* her.

July 1

Warning! #longpost ahead. You might want to grab a bowl of popcorn and a cuppa for this one, friends...

This post has been a long time coming.

In this picture, you can see my new reality. It's different than the Homestead and Hearth Ranch. Those posts, those images I took, they were curated for you. Before I put up a photo of my bedroom, I made the bed and cleared crumpled-up tissues and tweaked pillows and swept away trash and junk and clutter from the nightstand. There was always a heap of stuff in an off-screen corner. Stuff that would go back where it was or maybe build into a miniature hoard that I'd never show you. Oh, and? Those pictures? They had filters. All of them. Even the ones tagged #nofilter. I'm sorry. And it wasn't just filters, either. There was cropping and photoshopping and angles and so

141

much "magic" that you never actually saw what the Ranch looked like. At least, not on a normal day.

But the Ranch was my home, so of course I had messes, right? Now, it's little more than a studio. Sure, the brand has named it the Homestead Ranch, but if it were a homestead, it would have to be a home. No one lives there. I'm not telling you anything you don't actually know. Because that's the beauty of social media. We let ourselves believe that what we see in the little screen is reality. It gives us hope that we can be those people. Funny or beautiful or self sufficient. Right?

It was never me. I was born and raised in a western town with average parents. I was an average kid. I grew up and learned to cook and clean and take pretty pictures of pretty things. I learned about the ways of ranching from extensive research. None of it was innate in me. My goal was to do the thing my mom always told me I could do. Bring the world to my home. That's what homesteading was. Did I want to see beautiful art? Oh, I could make it with a canvas and painting supplies. Did I want to feel the softest couture ever? Have you ever tried your hand at crochet? ;) Did I want to smell a baby llama or watch the birth of a foal? I could do that too. My mother had great wisdom, but somewhere along the way I lost it.

I took all the things I learned to do—all the things I learned to be—and I monetized them. Not to pay the bills —though they paid the bills, of course. But to do more, do bigger, do prettier. By the time I was booted out of the ranch for a retreat, I had learned everything I needed to be a real *homesteader. Heck, they could have sent me into the wilds of Alaska, and I'd make it.*

But I was lost there for a while. I didn't have a computer or phone or the people I'd come to rely on to give me that immediate feedback, you see.

Some of you already found me. You tracked me down somehow, and that is pretty impressive. For those who don't know by now, I'm living on a real farm on the prairie in South Dakota. I've put all my hard fought knowledge to work in earnest. Not to throw away or snap a photo of. In fact, I'm writing this very post from a twenty-year-old computer in the Prairie Creek library's Reference Room. It's adorable here. Lots of oak and some dark wood. No shiplap, hah!

So, I don't have a smart phone right now. I'll get one again soon, but for this post, I had my trusty friend, Deb send along some of the footage she'd taken when she was up here with me.

The house in the background above? That's the little cottage where I work now. Yes, work! You're probably thinking it's a little sad for me to go from social media stardom to hourly wage work at a country bed and breakfast. You can feel that way, but I don't. In fact, I've never been happier.

Here at the Ryerson's Country Cottage—I wouldn't be me if I didn't throw in a little promo, eh? ;) —I milk goats and a cow. We make breakfast fresh from the farm to the table, just like I used to pretend.

It's not pretend here. It's early mornings every day. It's muddy boots and dirty hands and crusty overalls. It's manure and pig poop, too. But do you see that photo up there ^ ? I'm not alone here.

Not like I was for a long time.

The image above shows the back of me on the left. Obviously. The red hair is always a dead giveaway, I suppose. The man on the right? With the red flannel shirt and great hair and cute butt? He's my boyfriend, and my new business partner. Okay, okay. He's technically my boss. His name is Logan Ryerson, and if it wasn't for his kindness, I don't know where I'd be. Probably back in Austin trying to beg you to forgive me for something I thought I'd never forgive myself for.

But it's funny, forgiveness. Sometimes, you think you need it from the wrong folks. If you'll just swipe right once, you'll see the second photo in this post and the last one I'll put up for a while. See this gal in the sweater and linen pants and Velcro shoes? That's Junie Hayfield-Barnaby. She's Joanna's daughter, and you'd all love her. She's sweet as American pie, feisty as a Texas cheerleader coach, and as forgiving a Christian woman as there ever lived.

I go to church with Miss Junie every Sunday. Sometimes her daughter, Devery, comes along, too. We're great friends, the three of us, and that's another thing I've learned. Having millions of followers feels good. Can't say that it doesn't. And your support these past years? It's been real. I've felt that. It's carried me through the hard stuff, I promise you that.

But you know what? It's not friendship. Not like I've

got now. I'm not saying that so you'll hate me—rather I'm saying to remind you to think about what matters in your life. Is it getting those "likes"? Those "friend requests"? Or is it bickering over who gets the last buttery croissant before your morning walk with your bestie by your side? #justsayin

Anyway, Logan is wandering around the non-fiction section looking for books on how to install a clawfoot tub. I told him he could Google it, but... I'd better go now.

Thanks for tuning in to this little update. I hope God blesses you every day. And, you know what? I hope you go out there in living color. Don't make your bed. Don't rub makeup all over your face and hang your phone from a high-up angle to get that perfect selfie.

Just live.

To my fans, I'll miss you. To my family, I love you still (Dad, see you next month when you come up to SD for that trip!). To the Homestead and Hearth company, thank you.

Thank you for showing me who I always was.

#thecountrycottage #homesteaddreams #authenticity #reallife #imback #blessthismess

Epilogue

Kelly hit POST and then logged out of the account and turned off the computer. She bent over to pick up the small stack of books she'd accumulated—*Sewing for Dummies, Darn It! How to Darn and Mend*, and *Singer Sewing Machines, A Comprehensive History*.

"All finished?" Logan came up behind and he scooped his hand under her book stack. "Here, I've got those."

She smiled at him, and he leaned over the books and planted a soft kiss on Kelly's mouth. Every time they kissed, her insides lifted like she was in a free fall. A new sensation to be sure.

"Where to next?" Logan asked as the librarian checked them out.

"Home?" she answered. "We've got a lot to do still."

It was a little strange sharing a home with one's boyfriend when things were still early, but the relationship between Kelly and Logan was anything but fragile. And, it was anything but hot and heavy. They were on solid, new ground. Each kept to his and her own room. They made formal date plans on the weekends. And generally, they spent the days preparing the cottage for the next round of guests, turning beds and such, and planning the next restoration project. Logan had been firm that he hadn't wanted to renovate the place, and Kelly couldn't agree more. Instead, their goal was to bring the cottage into tip top shape as it might have been when Aunt Melba and Uncle Ned were in their prime. It was an homage to the family name, to the town, and to the idea that you really could do all those things that Kelly had only ever read on signs.

Love more.

Live simply.

And don't forget to *goof up* sometimes.

* * *

They arrived back at the cottage in the lazy part of the afternoon. Logan felt more like snuggling up on the sofa in front of a fire—even if it was summertime—than replacing the window pane in the mudroom.

But just as soon as he turned the truck onto the cottage drive, he saw a familiar white car sitting to the side of the barn.

"Who's that?" Kelly asked him. "Did you book anyone for tonight?"

"No," he replied, measuredly.

"Maybe it's a drop in. We've got the downstairs guest room vacant and ready. No big deal," she remarked easily.

But Logan wasn't so confident and calm. "It's not a drop in," he said.

Kelly lifted an eyebrow at him and then they both turned to see a short, stout blonde girl standing on the front stoop, arms crossed and staring at them like she could turn the world to ice.

"It's my sister."

* * *

Order the next story in the Prairie Creek Romances: The Thimble House, *featuring Mabel Ryerson and Griffin Dempsey, with guest appearances by all of your favorite Prairie Creek townsfolk.*

Also by Elizabeth Bromke

Prairie Creek:

The Country Cottage

The Thimble Shoppe

The Mulberry Market

The Picnic Spot

Other Series

Heirloom Island

Harbor Hills

Birch Harbor

Hickory Grove

Gull's Landing

Maplewood

Acknowledgments

For this book, I owe a debt of gratitude the fabulous Lisa Lee of Lisa Lee Edits. Thank you, Lisa, for being a friend and a terrific support. Your careful eye is ever invaluable, as is your ongoing encouragement.

Beth Attwood, thank you so much for polishing my stories and making *The Country Cottage* truly shine. You are so patient and knowledgable. I'd be lost without you!

I forged the idea and drew up the outline for this book long ago, and thank goodness. Because once it came time to write, life got crazy! A huge, *huge* thanks goes out to Leslie and Rich Engelhard, Ed, and my friends and family who offered great support on the homefront as I was facing both a book deadline and a closing deadline!

To my incredible ARC team—I am always so encouraged and inspired by your enthusiasm and positivity. Thank you for being my first readers and my cherished friends. Especially Marge, Mara, Lisa, Jeff, Ann, Pam, Karen, Terri, Susan, Gail, Elaine, Jan, MaryEllen, Chris, and Tony. Thank you!

Ed and Eddie, Winnie and Tuesday, always for you!

About the Author

Elizabeth Bromke writes women's fiction and contemporary romance. She lives in the mountains of northern Arizona with her husband, son, and their sweet dogs, Winnie and Tuesday.

Learn more about the author by visiting her website at elizabethbromke.com.

Made in the USA
Las Vegas, NV
15 April 2022

47510725R00087